# The Comedy Roast of Carroll O'Connor, Live Tonight at the Friars Club

## by Garrison Somers

# Blotter Books

Somers, Garrison 1957 - The Comedy Roast of Carroll O'Connor,
Live Tonight at the Friars Club
ISBN 979-8-9859878-5-0

Published in the United States by Blotter Books
an imprint of The Blotter Magazine, Inc.
1010 Hale Street, Durham, NC 27705
Printed and bound in the USA

To my friend John, who thinks nothing
of doing things for others without reward.

# 1

Some complete asshole of a production team member
is assigned the responsibility of hearing all of the complaints
about seating arrangement, even though four and a half weeks
prior to the event everyone attending and participating, a nearly
unmanageable subset of everyone attending, was sent a formal
letter of invitation, explanation, limitation and consternation on
cream-colored fifty-pound cardboard stock with a sketch of a
penguin in miniature black-tie and affixed with a red-carnation
boutonniere made out of some sort of origami type nonsense.
Although the intent is to look sort of classy, such details are
lost on those types who only appreciate pricy booze and green-
backs in high denominations. Most folks skimmed the invites to
ensure that there would be open bar. But a handful noticed, in
point of fact, that they're the same cards they used for the Y2K
party about two years ago. So naturally there are alcohol-fueled
complaints. And that poor yet complete asshole has to listen to
them and scribble with a silver Mark Cross pen on an official
looking pad of paper clipped to a clipboard all efficient-like even

though it cannot be said for certain that he is even writing in the English language, or that anyone he reports to gives a damn what the complaints are.  Who does that…person report to?  No one knows.  Maybe the Dean of Friars.  Maybe no one.

It's a goddamn mystery, if you ask me.

Furthermore, it smells here; like weed and flopsweat, spray air-freshener, old wet wool coats with a hint of fermented puke.  Which, it could be said, is the natural smell of the Friars Club, 55th halfway between Park and Mad, in the old Erdmann house.  Oddly enough, it's not a terrible odor, not for midtown New York.  It stinks, in a strange and good way, like your own home, that one you grew up in.  You don't know who thought it was a terrific idea putting a toilet in a tiny room next to the kitchen, where your dad hid while reading Sports Illustrated because the window behind the can was pretty good light, was propped open with an old broken-tipped drumstick from when he used to sit in with a bebop combo and no one bothered him here, so he could have a couple Reingold's, the bottles perched on the rim of the sink.  Even your dad's beer farts remind you of the old days when things were better, weren't they?  Better than now, anyhow.  That's how it is in the foyer of the club.  Pronounce that *foy-er*, or one of the older guys will throw a chunk of ice hooked right out of their scotch tumblers at you.  He hits you in the head with an ice fastball and the others have to ante up a five-spot for righteous aim.

It's a rule, one of many here in the western world.

Speaking of toilets, the guest of honor – who is not the roastee at all, surprisingly enough – is waiting in the blue room, so named because of all the foul language spoken there, like an awful Pentecost where God gives everyone the ability to speak in their own private tongues but everyone else understands full well

3

what they're saying. That's what cursing does for us – provides
a lingua-fucking-franca we all are able to easily grasp. They
curse in the blue room not just because they can, but because
it's a place for getting certain crap out of your system, in that
it is both soundproof and contains a private restroom. And the
guest of honor, the so-called "Old Man," one of the most senior
members of the Club, is locked in a death-struggle with his lower
gastrointestinal system, which won't provide him with that
particular relief he requires before he can go out and lambaste
the person actually being presented as the guest of honor as he
who is about to be roasted. It makes one think of those old Mu-
tual of Omaha Wild Kingdom episodes where Marlon waits in
the dusty olive-green Land Rover while Jim wrestles a
twenty-foot-long Reticulated Python bare-handed. The truth of
the matter is the Old Man only recently stopped his lifelong habit
of drinking six to ten daily cups of caffeinated coffee and his gut
has reacted to this biochemical alteration of the hi-test diuretic
norm by blocking him up like the brick-and-mortar wall in the
Cask of the Amontillado. I've never yelled at my gut to give
up the shit, so to speak, so I can't say precisely how it feels. He
seems full on distraught, though. His current consideration is
that it might be prudent to drill a second shaft, for air and food,
so that the miners might eventually be rescued. Read into that
what you will.

His chief hanger-on, a fellow alternately thought of as being
named Guy or Bud, but who is neither and is now paid a salary
somewhat less than handsome to provide the Old Man an
entourage, stands patiently at the door waiting to hear something,
a safe-word perhaps, that will send him into the bathroom to
assist in some horror-show way I don't even want to think about.
He is folding and refolding his handkerchief, preparing to use it

as a mask. Well, we all have our crosses to bear.

Outside, it is drizzling; that after-Labor Day New York City rain that isn't cleansing, in fact it makes you feel like wealthy people way up in the skyscrapers are emptying their bladders into the night air and that's what's falling on your head, B. J. fucking-Thomas. A video team of two people has set up shop outside the building, under one half-circle striped canvas awning, which provides little respite from the damp. They are waiting for some sort of red carpet like event. Tonight's roast is an anomaly. Nowadays the big roasts are typically held at a hotel, in one of their large ballrooms, so that all sorts of tickets may be sold or given away and the audiences can be part of the show. See how _____ reacts to hearing that _____ has three testicles? Isn't that grand? Aren't we lucky to have been here? But for some reason we are not privy to, this one is behind the closed doors of the Club, members in good standing only. No television, no Pay Per View, no residuals. Whose idea was that? What's the point, if not to milk such goings on for every nickel?

The producer – one Ms Joan Jones – is tucking her curly brown hair beneath a charcoal gray Kangol flatcap and doing a sound-check on her microphone. It is large and heavy, a lousy piece of technology two generations old, and the wet is messing with any fidelity it might still have. She looks out at wet New York and restrains an eye-roll, mumbles her frustration under her breath and the cameraman, whose name is, I swear to god, Antwerp Jones – no relation to Joan – asks her to repeat it even though he knows her mumbling is not part of the tech. prep.

Antwerp, so named by his father without fully considering the consequences, smiles and jiggles the jack to make the micro-phone squeal a moment into his headphones and the ear-piece that Joan is wearing. She hisses at the high-pitched noise and

5

gives him the stink-eye.

"Knock it off, 'Twerp.'" See what I mean? Terrible name. No, I don't care why. Awful.

So, the Jones's are here, standing out in the rain, because of the oddity of this particular roast. A comedy roast – when someone is elected to experience an all-in-good-fun no-holds-barred abuse-a-rama by their friends, cohorts and compatriots - a roasting - is not supposed to be private. Since its advent, comedy roasts have mutated from occasions among friends in some bar or restaurant, to invitation-only shenanigans at bigger restaurants, to hotel-ballroom televised enterprises. And now, when there is such dough-re-mi to be made from selling the rights to one of the major media conglomerates, so that they may broadcast them at some pay-per-view moment, then edit them for family viewing on consecutive evenings on a cable comedy channel (also owned by the conglomerate), this peculiar one is being pulled back in house, as it were. No cameras. No jiggly celebrities allowed to come and expose themselves for camera time. Oh, there will be a few, as guests of Club members. I mean, some guys just feel better when there are tits around them.

"There's no chance of us being…electrocuted?" Joan holds up the mic and interviews the wet air in front of her.

"Of course, there's a chance," says 'Twerp. It's true but unlikely, but like most tech guys he enjoys making the equipment seem magical to those less machine-knowledge inclined. "There's electricity and wires and water. Always possible."

"Should I be wearing gloves?"

"You mean rubber gloves?"

"Yes. Like dishwashing ones. Bright yellow. Those are safest." Joan shrugs and ducks inside her peacoat because water is dripping off the awning onto her neck. Miserable.

"Sure. That would be great," Antwerp smiles. He is not a fan of sarcasm, cynicism, snark, insult or blue. In fact, he rarely laughs where a smile will suffice. But he likes Joan's manner, her sense of humor, unsubtle and just a tad distant. It might be a crush, but only time will tell. He hopes he will get that time.

Joan peers out at the street, where the lights from passing cars and streetlamps reflect gloomily on the wet pavement. Just be there, their boss said. Someone comes by, ask them for a minute of their time. Get some footage. Funny stuff, you know?

You mean funny stuff like jokes? She asked this softly, because it was a legitimate question, but sounded dumb. Don't believe that there aren't any dumb questions. Yeah, he said. Jokes, pratfalls, etcetera. The whole comedy shit.

Yes, he actually said etcetera.

So she nodded and now they're here, and ready, and wet and waiting. For what and whom, it will soon be revealed.

"Tell me a joke," Antwerp says. He points the camera at her. She looks nice on camera.

"What?"

"A joke. You have to know a joke. Everyone knows a joke," he says flatly. "Tell me the best one you know."

Joan stands there, mic to mouth, actually struggling to re-member something funny, draws a blank. Then…

"There was this thing my dad used to do, like when we were all at the supper table."

"Who all?" Antwerp asks tentatively, knowing that he is interrupting.

"My mom and dad. My older sister Michelle and my little brother. Sitting around the table together."

"What is his name?"

7

"Robert."

"Is he smart? Roberts always seem to be smart."

Joan smiles. "Yes, and no. Good brain. Bad judgment. Used to ride his bicycle without a helmet."

"But that's everyone."

"Maybe, but not like this. He would do this thing where he got going and then stood up, one foot on the seat and one on the handlebars. Like it was a giant two-wheeled skateboard."

"Damn," said Antwerp. "Pretty badass, then."

"Dumbass" she corrects. "Knocked his two front teeth out." Joan taps her own teeth with a fingernail.

"When he was a kid, I assume?"

"Nope. When I was little. Right in front of us."

"Ouch."

"Yeah." Joan nods and feels the wet on her neck again. It's not cold, but it unlocks the clear memory, and gives her a shiver of nostalgia.

"So you're the middle kid." A statement of fact.

She tells him about how they would be eating, and every-one would be talking about what happened at school or after on the bus or just blabbing, all at the same time. Her folks didn't require everyone be quiet while they spoke, or not talk with their mouths full or anything like that. It was a free-for-all. The absolute best part about being a child in her family. Someone might want some mashed potatoes, they'd have to stand up and do a boarding-house reach to grab them. It should have been rude, but no one minded. Then after a while her dad would raise his hand, like a referee at a ballgame, and everyone would get quieter. This was his moment. And he would ask a question.

"Like what?" asked Antwerp, entranced.

"Is it colder in New York than it is in the summer?" Joan

says.

'Twerp frowns, and she snorts into the microphone.
"What?"

"Is it colder in New York than it is in the summer?"

"What does that even mean?"

"It means what it means. I have no idea. It makes no sense
at all, but it used to have Dad falling out, sliding out of his chair.
And that used to make us all laugh so hard milk came out our
noses. When I was a kid it was the funniest thing ever. Swear to
god."

There's a long pause, and nothing happens for that pause
– no cars, no talking, no pedestrians under too small, one rib
poking out, umbrellas scuffing by. It's a New York surprise.

"That's your best joke?" Antwerp asks.

"I guess." Joan replies and sighs loudly enough to pick it up
on the mic.

"Pretty good. Not great. Pretty good."

# 2

There are various alcoves and antechambers in the Erdmann
house, but none provide the privacy necessary to practice one's
trade. Hence a where-am-I-sunglass'd-at-night variation on an
eighties theme John K. sits in the arboretum of the IBM building
at 590 Madison, dressed in a tuxedo, but wearing an ancient J.
Peterman duster over the top. One of those waxed-canvas cow-
boy coats, for being out riding fence in one's mind while taking
New Jersey Transit to Piscataway. His boots are water stained
and sprung-heeled Tony Lamas that look far less expensive than
they were, have no place in a tuxedo ensemble, and they make
his disguise complete. The arboretum is mostly empty – a
couple of night-shift server monitors are taking an early bag
lunch, sitting on the concrete benches across the floor beneath
some leopard-spotted bamboo trees planted in manicured raised
beds – but the place is not locked shut because too many IBMers
use the high-rise's empty offices for their evening trysts under
the pretense of having international sales calls with Asia-Far
East. It's the view, you see. Look, baby – ooh, the sexy
Manhattan skyline. Pull some coffee-stained cushions from
couches outside executive conference rooms and lay them on
the sills and pretend that you're in the fifty-first floor club. Lay
them on the sills. See how that works, both times? It's all pretty

infantile and no one cares. Of course, there are actually people, employees, making calls to Asia. Why not? Call your nai nai and wish her a happy Thursday. The phone calls are all part of an enormous telecom budget that is nearly impossible to control and even harder to audit for credibility. John K. knows nothing about telecom, barely knows what the letters IBM stand for and doesn't care, and likes the damp darkness of the arboretum, with its echo-chamber acoustics. He does his wishful thinking tight five from his own bench as if he were someone squatting in the 53$^{rd}$ Street station raving at the voices in his head between downtown trains.

"How's everyone tonight. Really? Oh, bullshit. Fuck that noise. I don't believe you. What if I told you that we're out of Jim Beam? You would make more racket than that. You'd be pissed, wouldn't you? There would be pitchforks and torches and a mob. Don't worry, they're distilling more of it in the back as we speak. Three little guys with bare feet and long pointed beards. They're either leprechauns or lawyers from Kentucky. You don't think this place is paid for with your shitty dues, do you? Most of you are so skint that you're a year, eighteen months behind. Shit. I miss the old days, when home less was a goal, because of your wife's cooking..."

John K. knows that his thing, his persona, that of an aging hipster, is frayed at the edges. He's afraid at the edges, too, because the calls come fewer and farther between. When did he start 'aging'? Was he even paying attention back then, or still just woofing coke lines and swordfishing (that code name for finding middle-aged suburban housewives and convincing them to meet him for drinks and whatever in second-tier hotels, like the spartan single he has booked at the Drake across the

11

street.) Old is an uncomfortable tightrope walk if ever there was one. Being old? Funny. Even the hairy ears and diapers under your trousers. What isn't funny is getting old, now or ever, so pretending that you aren't is not fresh, not interesting. Pretending that you are pretending that it is new and unusual is…tricky. He's completely out there, on his own with it. His agent treats him differently now than when he first came up with the guys like Freddy and Jimmy and The Mook and Sad Art. Like he's C minus material. There are the calls with the occasional gig, but half-hearted – his agent preferring to leave long rambling messages rather than talking, knowing that John K. will probably not get the jobs and not wanting to listen to him gripe about that. Oh, he can still do clubs, but the math doesn't work very well. The places that want him cost and reward about even. The places that pay more don't want him, but he can come on in on list nights, take his chances. There are weeks where he knows he would do better…but, nope, there's nothing he can do other than this. Can't even wander too far away, because jokes don't travel. Something funny in New York is flat in…where? Mobile, Alabama? Is that even a real place? So if you leave, be ready to tweak the career. Is he good at anything else? A question that pops into his mind more frequently than thoughts of pussy in a fifteen year old D and D nerd. No, not even if you want fries with that. Imagine being completely unqualified to do a damned thing. Stand and make 'em laugh, or stand on the 53rd Street platform. Or go stand on the track.

John K. has an ancient, folded-over black-and-white composition notebook, of the kind that kids use in school. He calls it a 'commonplace book' and has it tucked in the pocket of his coat, with a fat stub of a carpenter's pencil, which is either interesting or ironic, he can't decide. On it is his last chance, his dream, his big idea, written in a kind of code that he has used since losing good material of his to a son-of-a-bitch he thought was a friend. That Bacardi rum sipping motherfucker. Never show anyone anything. This is his motto now, not that he has any boy scout bullshit in his life like mottos or mantras, morals or morale or mother's milk.

His big idea? A television show, of course, but a bleeding edge madhouse of one, something so off the wall that no one would ever listen past the first twenty seconds of it trapped on an elevator between floors, when the building is on fire. He envisions it, though, in that limp dick way we do when we're finally grasping our reality with both hands and a flashlight and a colonoscopy probe. Multiple cameras all rolling at once, pointed at a giant spotlit stage, where there are a battery of microphones and a dozen or two comics standing, waiting for the buzzer to start. It sounds and they start speaking into their mics. One bit after another, all at once and continual, a great and terrible Arnold Schoenberg atonal symphony of words, each standup doing their bits, the old stuff that always kills and then the untested new material, breaking in joke after joke, to the audience, trying to win them over while all of the others do the same, attempting to make yourself heard in a monstrous cacophony until they are selected out in some fashion. Maybe short, muscular bouncers with black executioner's hoods, or pretty women in sexy-policeman Halloween costumes. Eventually the field is cleared of riff-raff, leaving one comic there, with their mic, triumphant, exhausted, unable to go on, but must, next week, same bat-time, same bat-channel. Like those marathon dancers during the Depression that had to keep moving together on the floor to some horrid music, on and on, in order to win a cash prize to keep their families alive. Or politicians in Washington who must not yield the floor, keep on talking through the night, like that actor from It's a Wonderful Life, so that the kids get their summer camp. What is that word for endless gibberish? Filibuster. Only in this case, maybe judges use paintball guns to selectively remove the comics who don't keep up, don't make the grade. Splat – blue! Splat – red! All of the jokes and observations, insults and cruelties going at the same time, louder and louder, faster and slower, trying to be heard. Yes, yes. An audience would pay well to see judges putting a stop to that shit. Might want real guns, even. He is torn between two names for his show idea. Either 'Blast Man Standing,' or 'For God's Sake, Shut the Fuck Up.' They're both pretty good, he admits and shakes his head. It's a wild idea. No one would ever dare.

He sniffs, thoughtfully. His burnt nasal passages softly whistle. He doesn't do blow anymore – for a small handful of reasons. Can't afford the luxury of the misery. And a long while back he gifted over a fat payday to a plastic surgeon to repair his burnt-out septum under the guise of rhinoplasty. Fooling no one who knew him. He misses the good feeling that coke gave him. Oh, and quaaludes. They were…nice, too. The feeling is like waving at a pretty girl across a deep and terrible river full of crocodiles. Want? Yes. Need? Perhaps not so much.

It's time to go, he thinks as he checks his watch, a fifteen-dollar Rolex knockoff he bought downtown from a suitcase-vendor, just to have the experience of haggling for two bucks' savings. Everyone should do that, just once in their life. The watch is pretend gold, just like he is. Something that appears of value, which is only good if it's working right now.

"Do you think he has a penis? There's a question we hardly ever bother to bring up. I wonder why not? Is it because we don't want it

asked of us?  A kind of Geneva Convention of fair-use inquiries in modern civilization?  Hey, does so-and-so even have a dick?  Maybe that's
why he's such a complete ass.  He might have lost it, in some devas-
tating childhood illness that has no name in the medical world, because
we don't name things like that, because it's men.  If it's women, we give
it a name, but don't make medicine for it.  Of course.  'Where do you
think her vagina went?' they ask on the big pharma commercials during
the nightly news at suppertime.  'Oh, yes, well, she got the cumsquatus
infectus and now she doesn't have one.  Ask your doctor about analge-
sic balm.  Or, rather, vaginalgesic balm.  And get her a really big cork,
because otherwise all sorts of prolapse will happen, and no one wants
that.'  But a man losing his dick?  Can't happen!  Oh, hell no. Feed him
a blue pill, for pity's sake!"

# 3

Speaking of which, the guest of honor, only not really - the Old Man - has finally put paid to his GI blues, and stood up, buckled his trousers and is washing his hands at the sink, only to find that all of the paper towel dispensers are empty. He swings his hands in fart-fogged air. He remembers back when there was a little man sitting on a wooden chair in the corner whose job it was to hand out clean, dry, sparkling-white towels in restrooms throughout New York City. Those were the days. What did the application entail for a job like that? Do you have hand-eye coordination? Can you hold your breath and for how long? Did you bring a letter of recommendation from your coach? When was the last time you smiled? Or maybe bathroom attendant was an inherited position, like Hasidic rabbi or Samurai, passed from father to son, generation after generation, down through the ages. He misses those days; those racist, anti-Semitic, misogynistic, five-dollar-suit and bad haircut, cheap bastard, financial-cheating, class-distinct, blue-law, labor violent, burn the place down and walk away with the insurance, gentlemanly yet miserable days. Here's to fucking over the other guy to get a head, he raises his still-damp hand with a pretend glass in it.

Right now his wife would be wondering where he got to,
if she weren't dead these last seven years. Oh, it's been longer
than that, but the Old Man believes in the Old Testament rule of
not bothering with real numbers, just 'long time' code like seven
years of wandering the wilderness, or forty-days-and-nights or a
legion of demons versus hosts of angels. How the hell many is a
host, and how did the term come down etymologically to be the
one person with the microphone at one of these shindigs? The
Host with the Most. The Master of Ceremonies. The schlemiel
running the show.

His wife would know why. She was one smart cookie.
He'd gone down through the years as being a playboy, a lo-
thario, but he'd only married once and it stuck. That other stuff,
the offstage accusations of trysts and infidelities, was part of
the persona, fit right into his schtick. But it must have rung too
true, because he'd never gotten the big break – the television
show, the holiday special, the Dean-ship of the Friars. And that
hurt Margaret - 'Margarine' - so-called in his routines because
she wasn't the real thing, and you'd know it if you tasted her.
She said nothing though. Put up with it for so many years they
reached whatever that Old Testament number was for a shitload.
Or maybe she didn't say anything because she knew the truth
and didn't give a rat's ass about what people thought. And even
though he knew the truth, too, it dragged on him, because it
dragged on her.

A good old girl. He missed her. Had to remind himself
that she wasn't going to be sitting out at his table, and how much
that sucked. He finally wiped his still slightly damp hands on
the legs of his trousers, to hell with the knife-crease, and shoved
open the damned door.

17

What animal did you most look like when you were young? How many times did you run away from home as a kid and how many times did anyone care? Why weren't you popular in high-school? Was it the drama club or vocal workshop that ruined you, and saved you at the same time? Or was it chess? How badly did it go when you first got laid? And what went so very very wrong with your life that you ended up out here, in the rain? Joan and Antwerp are entertaining themselves with all those questions people ought to ask on a first date, over coffee or bad sushi, or standing in line to go to a club or movie. Why did everyone dance around the important stuff, wasting time and, more importantly, emotional capital, instead of getting to the crux of every human relationship – what do you think is funny? (You troubled, broken toy.) And they're doing it on camera with the tape rolling. Antwerp keeps making faces at her, too, so Joan can't help but smile. His explanation is that this will prepare her for being serious when she needs to be, during an actual interview.

Joan has all of the classic Daddy issues, including dating someone that, even though he had a full beard, wore the same crappy after shave as her dad. Under his arms. Yes, of course. On the other hand, Antwerp, in addition to being named after a Belgian seaport (which his mother repeatedly claimed was not on her mind when she filled out the birth certificate), was the first person in his middle school to take a shower after gym class, rather than just wiping off the sweat with a stiff, stinky towel, slamming shut his locker, and heading to his next class.

"What's wrong with that?" Joan asks. "Sounds like you were ahead of everyone else."

"Well, yeah," 'Twerp shakes his head, and fiddles with the camera for a moment. "But they all saw my cock."

"So?"

"In sixth grade it hadn't yet reached it's full…potential."

"Ah," Joan nods. "So has it?" She is blushing, but it's dark and wet and no one else knows.

"Since? I suppose so," Antwerp shrugs. He's mortified as well, but is a fair actor and makes it seem just another normal conversation between coworkers.

"No complaints?" She bites back a grin, knowing that he is absolutely about to bust a gasket, but not going to give in first and end this.

"Not formal ones," he says, playing the terrible game. "It just altered the playing field for a while."

"How?"

"Nicknames. Some pathetic, some very good."

"Tell me a very good one."

"'Good Golly, Miss Molly'," says Antwerp.

Joan frowns. "I don't get it."

"Think about it a moment."

It takes a few seconds. Joan's laugh comes out half-hiccup, half snort.

"Little Richard?"

"Yup."

Pregnant pause. Biting back a grin, again.

"Okay, that is pretty funny."

Antwerp nods and wipes the moisture from the lens of the camera with a piece of chamois.

John K. leans out of the IBM arboretum and looks up into the precipitation and shares a little foul language with the weather gods. He wants to hail a cab, but it's only rain and Madison is aimed in the wrong direction and oh by the way, taxis aren't

19

free. He fights the urge to turn around and go back inside the big building, or, standing at the corner waiting for the light, to make a left turn and head over to the hotel. He could order room service, a dry turkey and provolone cheese sandwich with some too-salty fries. A seven-dollar PBR, cold from the mini-fridge. Rustle up a deck of cards somewhere, play some Klondike solitaire until he gets sleepy or the sun comes up and housekeeping knocks at the door. Ridiculous, he cannot afford to not go, just blow off the gig, but it is a strong influence, his social anxiety. He can't afford cabs or seven-dollar cans of Pabst beer. What a conundrum! Like a magnet lodged in his bowels tugging him back away from everything that involves human interaction. Why didn't he choose some other path? What the fuck is wrong with Robert Frost, imagining the road less taken is somehow valuable, satisfying, adventurous, good, in all the ways our memories bleakly misrepresent reality. Idiot.

John K. sees himself reflected in a bank window, despite the darkness. Tall, heavy, hunch-shouldered. Haircut? Not too bad, but anyone with taste would lean over to the person sitting next to them at their table and make a tsk-tsk sound, seeing it was from one of those cheap speed-cut places. You're a bum, he tells the reflection. Three weeks from packing crate-sleeping beneath an overpass. Can't afford plane fare to balmy LA, so it's up to you, New York, New York. At least there'll be free food and drink at the Club. Hopefully, no one will tap him on the shoulder for his overdues.

He finally gets the blinking *Walk*, and begins to cross, scuffing through puddles on the pavement. In his peripheral vision there is movement and he automatically turns to look and steps aside at the same time, a naturally defensive nature, in this traffic-centric world of the Manhattan island. Coming towards him, fast, one of the Stuka dive-bombers of urban life, a bicycle messenger, wearing a shiny black Hefty bag over his head, with arms and neck hole, belted at the waist, one of the tricks of the trade in the underbelly economy of the Big Town. Skullcapped, begoggled, coach's whistle clenched between his teeth, lock and chain over the shoulder like a guerilla's bandolier. John K. would have thought that everyone wore helmets nowadays, but there are always rebels, rogues waging something against the someone.

The messenger gives a short burst on the whistle, shrill and crisp. The bicycle skids on the macadam to a stop but not before John K flinches and ducks, his hands over his head, anticipating absorbing all of the punishment of collision and roll on the tarmac; the New York City version of climbing under your desk when you're a kid to protect yourself from nuclear Armageddon. But, no. He stands, because he isn't actually hit by the bicyclist yet feels the embarrassment-heat in his face, then starts walking again in a too-late disdain for acknowledging the weird.

And the messenger follows him. Oh, shit.

"I know you," the messenger says, tugging his goggles down around his neck. "You're that guy."

"So are you," John K. mutters. "Everyone is someone."

"Yeah. Ha. I was right. You're funny. I mean I think I've seen you before. On TV?" The messenger rolls slowly alongside him.

It is an oddity, John K. thinks. After threatening to run him down, then complementing him, is he going to mug him?" From aboard the bicycle? Well, that will be disappointing for both of them. And now there's nothing to say. He's got nothing at all.

Once upon a time he blacked out during a bit. During a heckling. In Philadelphia, of course, where the concept of

21

talking to someone on stage that you paid to entertain you was probably invented. Guys leaning in the windows of Independence Hall, giving the Founding Fathers a ration of shit for not simply telling King George the Third to go fuck himself. This guy was sitting dead center of the front row, shaking his head at him at every joke, every observation. Just before the punchlines, like he knew what was coming. Maybe he did, the bits were not fresh, but that happens sometimes, and if it doesn't work for you, well, them's the breaks. John K. made the mistake of zoning out while he was talking and making extended eye-contact with him and the guy mouthed you really suck at him, slowly and animatedly, so it was definitely meant to be understood by him, even through the noise and smoke. John K. understood. So he pulled out of the tailspin, almost blinked like someone who'd taken a close call punch to the temple, and stopped the joke in mid-stride. Stood there, like he was lost. And he was. The guy had derailed his train of thought. After a very long pause, during which some folks were actually twittering because they thought the quiet was funny enough, John K. actually said hang on a sec., and started something different, something he'd only recently been working on. Really rough stuff, ugly and immature, and filthy as hell. The guy in front-center was frowning, and it had to be because he knew that the joke was not what had been originally, that there was no way this new thing was even remotely connected to anything he'd done before.

"We're lazier than cats. You know that old chestnut that cats sleep eighteen hours a day, and then run in circles, purposefully try and trip you when you're walking, or yowl at the darkness the other six. It's true, but we're worse. Humans are way worse. We can't even make ourselves happy. At least cats can lick their own dicks. Humans are stuck, with little dicks, like you are…" and he pointed at the man, and got the laughs, like that first rain spattering against your windshield when you're driving. "Can't lick our dicks, can't shove them up our own asses, like many of you here are silently wishing right now you could. And we're always waiting for someone to make us laugh. Good luck. Or maybe there was this Darwinian thing that happened back during the lonely, cold, dark Ice Age. Sitting around the fire, all the grubs and nuts gnawed clean, bored because the sun went down and the fire was burning itself out and there was no television and no comedy club to go to. Everyone who could, just sitting there sucking their own dicks, or bending them around and jamming them up their ass. Everyone else, all the women and children, doing dishes or sleeping or watching this strangeness by fucking flickering firelight. And those who were busy sucking their own dicks died of natural causes, way back before recorded time, because they were attacked by saber-toothed lions while otherwise occupied. Although I must admit it seems a bit odd that being eaten by a lion while you're eating yourself is called natural causes. Anyway, the lesson, or at least one of them is that when you're sucking someone else's dick you have an extra pair of ears, patiently waiting and listening for things like Mom at the bedroom door. Or a saber-toothed lion. And all those prehistoric solo fliers didn't hear someone say, 'hey, Oog,' – they're always named Oog, or Glug or Glyph-something because that's the noise you make when you can suck your own dick – 'hey, Oog, you probably want to quit that dick-sucking for a moment, on account of there's a saber-toothed lion somewhere close.' And most of the Oogs of the world missed that message. I could be wrong, of course. It could just be the cold that got them. Anyway, we're what's left. Little dicks who pay to laugh."

And that should have been that. But the guy wasn't done. He said, completely audibly, somehow, over the actual laughter that the unfermented bit is getting – not killing but certainly not dying – is that all you got? Dick jokes? And John K. stood there, in awe of something so well done. He'd been had by a master. The nearly perfect heckle.

And for reasons he still cannot quite fathom, because you don't pick a fight with your audience – it's the worst thing you can do, to admit that someone's under your skin – he flipped the bird at the guy in the front row. And stood there, defiant. The guy got up, and he wasn't very big, not particularly scary, but when he made to clamber up on stage, John K. scooted for the wings, even though he still had a good two or three minutes left of his time, if not of material. Didn't look over to see if the stagehands got Philadelphia little-dick back in his seat or showed him the door.

"Maybe," he says to the messenger, who looks over at him, gives him the up-and-down, his unwhiskered face dripping rainwater, his canvas duster, the boots. He is older than John K.'s first thought that he is probably not even old enough to drive, if he cared to switch to internal combustion. It's the strange streetlamps and the reflections off the street that made him young. The light is flattering. He wonders if he looks good, too.

"So, like what do you do?" asks the messenger.

It's a normal question, John K. thinks. What do I do? So why am I at a loss, defensive. Why did you think I was famous if you don't know where you've seen me?

And he also hesitates because he doesn't just want to say stand-up because it's so stupid sounding. I do stand-up. It opens up that childish retort 'doesn't everyone?'

"I'm supposed to be a comic," he says after two or three

beats – poor timing! - as they are now moving slowly down the sidewalk on Madison. The messenger can magically balance himself on his bike, without putting his feet down or moving forward much. His high-top canvas sneakers are wet from splash, though, and worn out, like a little kid makes his shoes by wearing them every day, all day. Balancing buys them a few extra moments of life. This must be something you learn when you spend a lot of time on a bike. "Lately, though, I'm in a rut."

"Not feeling it?" asks the messenger. "I know what you mean. Maybe it's not something you can force."

"What the fuck do you know about comedy?" The question just leaps out, all nasty and mean like that. John K. knows what is wrong with the question, the mood he is always in, and his own world, one of confrontation and hate-humor. It's that constant question, spinning round and round in his skull, looking for a way out. The one he always asks. The query that is reflected, deflected in his bits.

The young man on the bike doesn't seem to mind, though, that John K. has revealed some dark aspect of himself.

"I know a little. I know what I like, and what I don't like."

"What do you not like?" He may only get one try, and that feels like the truer test.

The messenger finally puts a foot down and stops rolling. John K. stops walking.

"I don't like sarcasm or being an asshole. Anyone can be mean, and so most people are, like it's a default mentality to have. That rut we ride in. They say when we're kids that it takes more muscles to frown than smile, but it seems harder to smile. I suppose there's less in the world to smile about."

John K. feels one crossing his own face at the man's words. They are innocent, and he wants to respond See? That's why

25

comedy is difficult.

"I don't like cynicism. I find that most people are wrong when they think they're world-wise or -weary. They know very little about the whole world. Wittiness could be fun, but it's usually a dog-pile – someone finding someone weaker than them and chewing them up. Caustic humor – insults and stuff – is what bullies do. It's more sad than funny. Puns are hard, and most people think it's cheap wordplay. I challenge them to find good puns."

The messenger knows he's been monologuing and shakes his head.

"I don't know, I haven't given it a lot of thought," he says with a sheepish grin.

John K. realizes that the guy is being sincere with him. This is new, astonishing, and he doesn't know what to do with the moment. Usually, such a moment requires a scene-closing pie in the face, because that's what you do with sincerity. You trip it into the mud for the cheap laugh and tension-release. You pants it. You boop it on the nose. Society can't handle the sincere, kind person, because he makes us feel smaller, lesser, more like the helpless piles of shit that we are. So break out the seltzer. But this time, John K. decides to leave it on the shelf, and he can't say exactly why.

He very much wants to know the answers to such questions.

"You've just described everything I do. All of the tools in the toolbox," he says, as if they are sitting in someone's living room, listening to jazz on the hi-fi.

"Yep. Sorry about that."

"What then?" John K. asks, as a passing car hits a puddle and he jumps to keep from being splashed. "What do I do?"

"Something different. There's always something different,"

the messenger says.

"I'm on my way to a gig right now," John K. says, almost plaintively. "I'm one of the...roasters."

"I don't know what that is."

"Yeah." John K. stops walking. It is quiet here, in that way that the city sometimes gets, when everyone is out of the weather, and the traffic lights have trapped all of the cars and trucks somewhere else. It is almost peaceful. What the hell is a roast? But he doesn't explain. It would take too long, and still it wouldn't make much sense. A moment of madness in an already crazy world.

"It's like beating someone up for being themselves. With words. By invitation only."

"Once I hit someone with my bike." The messenger circumscribes a careful path around him. "Only time I ever ran a pedestrian down. Not too long ago, either. It was midday, not gloomy like now. No one can teach you that when you're in a hurry, you have to think beyond the road in front of you, to the next group of people, cars, trucks. Doors sometimes open. People step into the street against the light, or with it but not looking to see if everything is clear. They don't see me on my bicycle, only cars and cabs and other vehicles. A whistle does some good, but it's shrill and out of most folks' 'pay attention' range of hearing. So this guy, maybe your age, in a suit and coat, carrying a briefcase and a paper cup of coffee, walked right in front of me. No time to swerve, no room either because I would have hit someone else if not this guy. You know how you make decisions like that? Who's more guilty? Who deserves what's coming?"

"I suppose," says John K.

"Nope," the messenger corrects him. "You just keep going the way you originally planned. There's no minor correction for

27

error. No Hollywood last-minute Oh, my god, moment. Just straight ahead. Now, this guy is the one who walked in front of me. What did he deserve? Me to plow him down? Maybe. Or maybe he was having an awful, exhausting day already and lacked the attention to the details in his world, the situational awareness. And I clobbered him. We both went down, hard, on our hands and knees and faces. Him under me, me under the bike as it flipped me over the handlebars."

"I tried to roll off of him, but my bike was laying sideways on me and tangled, front tire turned and twisted. So the fellow I hit is groaning and I'm groaning and and suddenly there's helping hands, pulling the bike off and strong hands under my arms, lifting me and I thought how it was really nice but suddenly someone kicked me in the gut. With their shoe. The hands under my arms threw me on the pavement again."

"What the fuck," John K. said.

"What the actual fuck, indeed," said the messenger. "The people who saw the accident, and there were quite a few as it was lunchtime in Manhattan and good folks were piled up at every intersection trying to cross this way or that, scurrying to and fro, decided that I was at fault for running down a poor son of a bitch with my bike. A purposeful and heinous act of assault on a pedestrian. A hit and…what? I don't know. But they kicked me and punched me and stomped on my bike tire spokes with their Thom McAns and helped up the man I'd collided with from the street and brushed him off, picked up his briefcase and what they could of his newspaper. In the old days, what I got was called an ass-whipping. For the circumstances of just being me."

John K. stops on the sidewalk at the corner of Fifty-fifth and Mad. The lesson is not lost on him, but he doesn't know what to say.

"I gotta go this way," he says to the young man on the bike. He wants to know how the man got away. A mob is a mob. Was this the same bicycle, or did he leave it behind when he somehow broke free. Did the cops come and arrest him, or rescue him? But he didn't have time or know this person well enough. And part of him - the cynical, sarcastic, caustic, damaged part of him – wasn't sure he was truly interested enough to take a few more minutes, because that's all he had before he needed to get to the Friars. Just a handful of minutes. Sorry.

"So when do you gotta be there?"

"It begins at ten."

"Why so late?"

"I don't know. It's just the way it is. A late-night lifestyle."

"So you've got some time, then," says the young man.

John K. looks at the face of his Faux-lex. He can't see it. He is not even sure it's still telling time at all. He shakes it, hoping for some new information. The messenger laughs. See, you are a comedian.

"It's only about 8:30, man. Let's get a drink, and you can ask me the questions." The messenger points at the small orange neon sign over a door that marks a hole-in-the-wall neighborhood pub. Strange. There's no neighborhood here, John K. thought. Just cold, distant businesses. Aliens. As enigmatic a name for a drinking establishment as anything they have down in Soho.

The young man hops off his bike at the door and hoists it onto his shoulder. The padlock and heavy chain he wears jangle as they push bumpily inside.

◆◆◆

29

# 4

Joan has to pee. Camera still rolling.

"I gotta whiz," she whispers into the microphone, so Antwerp can only just hear her in his earphones, then hands it to him and goes over to the door of the Club. In a few moments she has returned.

"That was quick," the cameraman says, recording...everything. "No lines for the ladies' room?"

"No ladies' room. Do you believe that shit?"

"Of course there's a ladies' room," Antwerp says. "It's a public place."

"That's not what the guy said."

"What guy?"

"I don't know. Some guy."

"Ah."

They look at each other and recognize what's happened. It's a private club. Not a public place. Probably don't have a ladies' room, the chauvinist bastards. Fuck 'em.

"There's a McDonalds down Third," Antwerp offers. It's a lame thing to say, and he knows it. He pulls out the keys to the minivan, which is pointed towards Madison, and through which she would have to continue to go down Fifth a couple of blocks, then come back to Third in order to pull over with the hazards blinking and try to run into the Mickey D's to piss. It's a non-starter. Joan sighs. New York sometimes blows.

"Piss in the van." He turns off the camera. Sometimes you don't film.

Joan shakes her head, not in disagreement, but with regret that this is what has to happen. It's dark, getting cold, and the rain feels like it's picking up, which makes the pee-urge worse, and she needs to hurry and get it over with and come back here and stand some more. Why? There's no one here, even though this thing is supposed to start soon. Is no one coming? Did all the funny old men come early? Maybe there is some kind of dinner bullshit inside, baked catered chicken or fish with a side of peas-n-carrots. Or is there a house-chef who has a way with wagyu beef tips and creamed spinach that makes you want to leave home and never return. Who knows? It's a fucking private club, with no ladies' room.

There's a Big-Gulp plastic cup in the console, and she takes it and does what needs be done, carefully setting the cup on the ground beside the van when she is done. Steam rises. That's a smoking gun if ever there was one, Joan thinks, and considers tipping the mess over with the toe of her shoe so that it can become one with the New York City urine festival, but doesn't.

As she shakes her head and takes the mic back from Antwerp, a car pulls up to the curb in front of the Club. She regrets her three-day-hair and tucks the Kangol in her back pocket.

"Camera," she hisses. "Do I look OK?"

"Like a wet cat," Antwerp says, once more hefting the JVC to his shoulder. "Perfect. Rolling...."

The passenger door of the automobile opens, and a man gets out. Older, big but stoop-shouldered, with a brushy mustache a full decade or more out of style, like he once broke into Watergate or played in a two-lead-guitars rock band. He's wearing a tan London Fog raincoat and a tweed stalker hat pulled low over his brow and carries an umbrella, which he pops open with a button. Joan moves forward out from under the awning, waiting for the man to open the back door and release the celebrity.

But he doesn't. He leans the open umbrella into the damp air and walks her direction, to the front door. The car pulls away. Shit, Joan thinks. Who is this? With no time to consider, she steps up to the man, just a bit taller than she is. She holds up the microphone expectantly.

And he doesn't stop.

"Excuse me, sir," she says. "I'm with _____ TV news. Do you have a moment? We'd like to interview you. Ask a few questions?" Jeez, that was desperate. She cannot seem to make her voice behave, it sounds like a sorority girl on campus radio. All that's missing is the hiccup-laugh.

He stops, gives her a look like he's not certain she's telling the truth. In a quantum moment of enlightenment, she decides that if he reaches for his wallet to give her a homeless-dollar, she's going to quit the business. Thank god, Antwerp flips on the camera floodlight, bathing the space with an ugly mix of white-glare and shadow. It doesn't help how she feels she looks, but it gives her story credibility.

"Sure, sure," the man grumbles. His voice is gravel-pit deep, like it's been broken by years of cigar smoke and brown liquor. And age. He's not young, she can see, or else that's the lousy lighting. "Whataya got?"

"You're here for the Roast?"

"'course." And he stands there, frowning, his umbrella dripping on her outstretched arm. Nothing else to offer. She stumbles over her next question.

"Are you a friend of the, the roasted?"

"Cardinal O'Connor?" he says, deadpan. "New York Archdiocese."

"Who? What?"

"Isn't that who is being roasted tonight?" says Mustache. "That's why I came. I'm here seeking revenge for Joan of Arc."

Joan stands there, mic extended. The man doesn't even blink.

"You're kidding, right?"

"Nah."

"Um, well, thanks, then." And she lowers the microphone before the water running over her arm shorts the damned thing out.

But the man stands there, still frowning at her. He wipes at his mustache with the sleeve of his raincoat, putting more water on than taking away.

"You know what, sis?" the man says, his words so low and slow and Bogart scratchy it's difficult to tell if it's the way he means to sound, or if he's making himself imitate a record playing on the wrong speed. "You shouldn't give up, just because I'm being a sonofabitch."

"I'm sorry?" She's puzzled. She's never been called 'sis' before, nor was she expecting an impromptu education.

"Don't put up with it. My crap, that is. If you're gonna do it right, you gotta be tenacious. Get in my face with that microphone."

"OK. What then?" Joan asks. Her head is cold and wet. It feels like her nose is running, but she cannot sniffle right now, that would be the worst, like she's about to cry. She prays it's not. It's snot, she smiles. The moment feels surreal. Antwerp has slowly moved closer, behind and to her left, not helping

33

really but still on her side - never turning off the camera. The shadows from the focus floodlight change the man's look, molding his features like something from an old Hammer film. Older, younger again, chiseled, putty-like. He doesn't smile behind that brilliant mustache. Even in this light, or lack thereof, his eyes are a transparent blue.

"You know that you get more words from someone with open-ended questions. Didn't they teach that in journalism school? Like, 'why do I bother to come to things like this, instead of staying home and watching something good on television, like the Mets or the Met?' Don't ask me something I can answer with a yes, or, because it's more likely, a no. And never accept an 'I don't know.' Push me back. Ruffle my feathers. Try again." He points at the microphone, nods his head.

"Who are you and why are you here?" Joan feels her face flush, because she just let the cat out of the bag. Who even says 'ruffle my feathers'? She has no clue who this odd fellow is.

"I'm an assassin and I'm here to take out the trash," the man says matter-of-factly into the camera.

"Which trash?" she asks without skipping a beat.

"Heh. Good one," the man's grumble-voice replies in a way that emphasized that he is neither laughing nor thought it was a good one. He turns his head and coughs, a soggy rattle in his chest. "Never mind. I'm nobody. A cat burglar. Second storey man. Just here to see the show."

"Small show. You're the only person that's come since we got here."

"I dunno," the mustached man doesn't shrug. "That's weird. Must be a back entrance, then."

"Why do you think the Friars made this occasion private?"

"Another good question. Maybe someone thinks it wasn't

for public consumption. Or it's what they call a practice run. Something to do, but not share with the mob. There's always those guys who want to see what other guys have in their tool-box. See if it's any good."

"Is it ever?"

"I suppose it depends on who you ask. A roast is mostly a way of blowing off steam, I think. You know, it's not hard to make people laugh. Humor is fucked up, pardon me, because it's looking for something in the worst of us, and turning it upside-down. Finding the funny in things that would otherwise make you cry, go catatonic, punch the shit out of someone or bleed from the ears." He tilts the umbrella back, finally, so that he is now also getting wet. Mist drips on his face, sparkles in his mustache. "Making someone laugh while someone else cries is easy. The problem is you have to be messed up a lot to want to look so hard at the things that might make you miserable or fly into a rage. We think we want to stop and stare at the car wreck on the side of the road, but we really don't. Our supposedly natural curiosity is balanced by a self-protection instinct to keep our sanity intact. Comics are the opposite of self-protective. They embrace the madness. And the roast permits the maddest of it all, a constant barrage of barbs and jabs. Just because it's humorous doesn't mean it amuses."

"What makes you laugh?"

"Right now? Oh, shit. Nothing. Seriously, nobody. I'm in a happiness recession. A black hole of the blues. Hey, that's pretty good…" The mustache wiggles from side to side, drips.

"So you're hoping that this will break you out of that?"

"Maybe. Hope might be the wrong word. Or just search-ing?"

"So who are you hear to see? Anyone in particular?"

"John K."

"Is he your favorite?"

"Not really."

"Why don't you like him?"

"I like him well enough. He's my son." He gives her an eyebrow-up look that says see how you wheedled this out of me? Good for you.

"I've heard of him," Joan says, struck by the suddenly interesting aspect of this. She's also actually pleased with herself that she is not just interviewing this man, throwing out questions, but participating in the conversation. "He's OK. I mean, I've heard he's good."

"Faintest praise," says the mustached man. "In comedy you either kill or die. There is no OK."

"You sound like Mister Miyagi," says Joan with a crooked smile.

"Who?"

"The man in that movie about learning karate."

"Yeah. No, I never saw it."

"But you know what I'm talking about, right?" Joan persists. "Reasonably famous pop culture stuff. It's not like you have to see something to be aware of it."

The man finally smiles back. It is a surprisingly heartening smile.

"I have a friend who says something like that. That you can't say you don't know who the Rolling Stones are if you've ever been in an elevator. If you do, you're revealing to the world that you're a liar. It's weaponized ignorance."

"So, Mister Miyagi?"

"Yeah, yeah. But my point to him is that you have to pay attention to something to really get it. Read the difficult books.

Listen to the dissonant music, even if doing so hurts or is hateful to you. It's interesting you think of me as a teacher. A sensei. I think my son would disagree, formally and vehemently. But we'll see. If he gets here, we'll see." And the man bows his head to her and nods, which she understands is his way of saying he would now like to go inside.

"Thank you for this," Joan says. "For taking time right now with me."

"Young lady, you are welcome." He puts the umbrella back up over his head and turns, walking to the front door.

"Wait," Joan says. "I never asked. Who are you?"

But the man pulls the door open and enters without saying.

The Old Man is finally in his seat, alone - he has chased away his hanger-on - with a crystal tumbler full of martinis, dirty, about three or four drinks' worth of alcohol. He doesn't care for the foolishness of cocktails, the presentation of refresh-ment. Put the fucking booze in a container and serve it, for crap's sake. Efficiency in consumption. Then leave me alone for a while, if you please. He looks around the room, but the little lamps on the tables create a glare that precludes him from being certain that he's seeing anyone he recognizes. Oh, the fuckers are out there, but hiding in the darkness, but others are, too. A lot of younger members, with their younger members. Idiots, imbeciles, morons, what have you.

His table's location is strategic – close enough to watch the event, far enough away that he isn't an easy target. Years of experience have given him clarity on this, sometimes you're asked to row when you don't want to be in the boat in the first place.

He fiddles with his fork, ready to fling it at a moment's

notice at anyone invading his space.  He's in a normal rotten
mood – his gut has settled down, finally, but the dinner plate
before him is untouched, cold fish with a now-jelled rice
*pee-loaf.*  There is a jazz trio perched in a corner of the room,
cramped together like they're busking in a subway car filled with
passengers who just want to get home.  It was somebody's
terrible idea, implemented anyhow.

He can see the main table, but there is no one there, yet.
The master-of-ceremonies must be upstairs somewhere, sorting
his notes, picking his nose, shaving his nuts, some damnfool
thing.  And the roastee – he who shall regret his fame – hasn't
arrived.  If he had, there would be the typical buzz around the
room, a fetid electricity of anticipation.  So he sips his drink –
this is a time-honored act and he well knows how to pace himself.  Quite a few people here will mistake their drunkenness for
talent and skill.  The stories won't be legendary, but they will be
told anyway, until no one is left who cares to hear them.

"Hiya, old pal."

The Old Man accidentally gulps salty gin and it almost goes
down the wrong pipe.  Son of a bitch.  He braces for a clap on
the back that, thankfully doesn't come.

"How you doing?  Haven't seen you around much.  I'm
glad you're here."

He came up from behind, the Old Man thinks.  That's why I
didn't see him.  Like a MiG on my six.  The Dean of Friars, and
his wet hands and his bad breath.  Fuck me.  He swallows again
and forces himself to not cough.  He won't give the bastard the
satisfaction of having surprised him.

"Hey, buddy.  You mean I aint dead yet, and I'll see if I can
get a second opinion," he says, and gives a rumbly fake chuckle,
which helps clear the gin out of his gullet.  And now, he is fully

aware, he has to talk; to share a friendliness with this man that he doesn't feel. He may even have to accept a gift, which happens almost immediately, when the Dean of Friars asks if he may sit with the Old Man for a moment and catch his breath, he's just so busy tonight and everything is going smoothly but for the grace of god, and I see you haven't touched your meal, let me get you a fresh plate, the trout almondine is excellent for being out of season – flew it in, no expense spared.

The Dean waves his hand like the king on a balcony at Buckingham and a contract white-shirted waitstaff pops up like magic and prepares to scamper off to get the Old Man another plate of food but is stopped by the hanger-on – Buddy or Guy or whatever it is, and he shakes his head at the waiter and goes to the kitchen himself to get more of what the Old Man doesn't want any of.

Holy shit. Why can't I have a pack of Bicycles, a fresh drink and a stinky Macanudo and just sit here quietly playing Klondike?

Go away! he wishes silently to the petulant gods, but nothing like that ever comes true.

The Old Man prides himself for being able to listen to other people's gibberish without eye-rolling, while he's got an interior frustration-monologue going on, and still being able to pay reasonable attention to what's happening around him. It's a gift, like some kind of radar. And, of course the Dean of Friars puts this to the test.

"You're the one everyone wants to see, you know that, doncha?" The Dean gives him a big old butt-smooch. The Old Man deflects it back over the net.

"Oh, I appreciate you're saying so, but there's a heck of a lot of great talent here tonight." Again, he has no fucking idea who's here tonight, because of the glare of the table lamps. Probably the usual suspects, here for dinner and the open bar, and maybe one or two surprises. That's normal fare for this kind of shindig.

And speaking of fare, the new plate of dinner arrives, and is quietly set before him. The Old Man ignores it. Tries to, anyhow.

"Eat, my friend. We all have to keep up our strength."

The Old Man picks up his trusty fork, and flakes off a bit of fish, nibbles at it, pretends he enjoys it with great relish. Yummy, you prick.

"Miserable out, isn't it," says the Dean of Friars. "You can always tell when summer is over in the City."

The Old Man nods, his mouth not remotely full of food, but he pretends that it is so he needn't respond to this sort of insipidness. We're really going to talk about the weather?

"They want to know why we didn't make this a show."

"They who?"

"Everyone," says the Dean.

"My friend, I say this with all respect to our colleagues in the so-called industry, but fuck 'em."

"Some of the members are asking why they weren't consulted."

"It's not a democracy."

"Still...." The Dean is a bit of a wishy-washy old carny, from back when it was still something to be upstate all summer, emceeing and schmeering his light-blue five minutes over an evening of dancing with a nobody big band. Signed photos for sale in the back. Shaking hands, kissing cheeks, silly stuff from back before it all got so...unpredictable. But he's almost as old as the Old Man, and there are so few of his peers left around who aren't wearing terrycloth bathrobes and paper slippers, sitting in common rooms watching gameshows all day.

Anyone who cares about televising this can only be in it for the publicity, and that means he doesn't care what they like or don't like. What are they going to do, boycott the Club? Steal bottles of Chivas to trade for blow with their hoodlum friends? OK, that last is actually plausible, comics are desperate lunatics.

The Dean mentions a name, a funny enough, not so young fellow, but mostly a one-trick pony. Do you know him, he asks the Old Man.

"Sure."

"Do you like him?"

It's the wrong question, the Old Man muses. Like means so many things. Do I like when he buys my drinks? Do I like the fawning over me that he does, the kissing of the ring as a sign of respect? Do I like his work? Do I think he's funny, and not just a flash in the pan? Do I like his odds of having staying power, being successful enough to make it past the first bright appreciative glow of fame without melting down and drinking, fucking or snorting himself to death?

"Sure," he repeats, because it saves time. He briefly supposes that he would like him, if he gave a shit about him at all. Life often feels to him the way it did in high school, so long ago. There is so much going on that it is impossible to pay attention to most of it. Thank god most of the stuff he ignores seems to be boring.

"His father is here," the Dean says, and the Old Man almost feels like he needs to shake his head like a cartoon character and hear the audible loose marbles in a coffee can rattling in order to remain engaged with the conversation. Whose father, he doesn't ask, partly because he remembers and partly because please, I

41

don't care!

"Hmm," he says after stuffing a bit of the rice pilauf in his face, so he won't have to have an opinion or response he cannot muster. Hey, this really isn't as terrible as I thought it was going to be. Imagine that!

"Do you know who his father is?" and the Dean says a name of modest fame in the industry. Yeah, maybe he knows him. A radio guy from Cleveland. An actual disk jockey voice, from back in the day when there were no extra pairs of hands doing the spinning. Or maybe that was someone else. Funny. With a different last name. Oh, well. No I don't know who his father is.

The Dean explains who John K.'s father is. Oh. Yeah. Him I know.

"I wasn't even certain he was a member of the Club." The Dean chortles, which is something so very out of fashion to do that the Old Man sighs and accidentally coughs out some of the rice onto his plate, and the table. He shrugs his apology. The Dean barely notices. "It turns out that he isn't, so I gave him a pass to get in tonight."

"Good for you," says the Old Man, as if he is talking to a twelve-year-old kid who successfully raked the front yard clear of leaves without being told.

Inside the heavy oak door of the bar named Aliens there is nowhere for the bicycle messenger to park his steed. He thought he might just lower it off his shoulder and set it on the floor, but there is a stool by the door and then a strange little outcropping half-wall that serves no purpose John K. can discern other to make the place more cluttered than it already is. Café tables and chairs, made of iron, the kind you might find on a corner in Paris where hard workers take another day off and drink coffee with brown sugar. They are heavy, so that even when no one is sitting in them, they are in the way. The dive is not full, but not empty, either; a thin little cavern with one side dedicated to the distribution of beverages and the other for perching to drink them. No wait staff – you have to get your own lazy ass up to the bar and place your orders. Which is what they do. The bartender is tall, white shirted and stoop-shouldered and gives them both a what the hell do you want look. It's perfect.

"I can't leave it outside," says the messenger.

"Against the wall, then. Over there," points the bartender and the young man follows the finger, locking the front and back wheels together with the chain to one of the iron stools.

"Habit," he explains to John K., who has already ordered two Piels drafts and carried them over. It is awful with low-alcohol content, sour stuff lacking both hops and time, but familiar to his tastebuds. The messenger takes a slug and grimaces. So bad.

"Habit," says John K. and the two of them smile at each other.

"What's your name?" asks the messenger.

"John." John K. says. It sounds ridiculous to say, in a bar in New York. He shakes his head. "What's yours?"

"Apache."

"Really?" asks John. "Apache?"

"No. But it'll do until something better comes along."

A television is on over the bar, and they sit and sip their beers and watch a moment. The room is both quiet and noisy. It reminds John K. of a lot of stand-up joints, where you have to work a half-hearted room from a corner with a crummy microphone, for people who aren't even sure what the hell you're trying to do, having no interest in being entertained at all.

"So you really have to be somewhere at ten?" asks Apache.

"I really do. At nine. Split the difference, nine-thirty." John K. says. He shakes his wristwatch yet again and holds it to his ear theatrically. "Can you please keep an eye on the time for me?"

"What is so important that you have to do it late at night like that? You a musician?"

"Ha," John K. barks a laugh. "Nothing that decent."

"What then? You're not in the NBA. A little too scruffy to be in the Army. Too much of you to be a dancer on Broadway. You don't look like a politician or a mafiosi don. Not with those shit-kickers." He taps John. K.'s boot with the toe of his soggy sneaker.

"I'm a comic. Really."

"I thought you were kidding before. Don't tell me you can tell jokes."

"No, nothing like that. Or something, maybe." John pauses, actually thinking about it. "I observe things. People, how they live, what they think. Society. The oddities and quirks in what is otherwise normal existence. Sometimes it makes people laugh."

"Sounds to me more like you're a philosopher," says Apache.

John K. rubs the condensation on the side of his glass until it drips from his fingers. He considers the idea.

"Maybe. Maybe we're just the modern version of philosophers. Responsible for telling things as we see them. Or the reincarnation of Diogenes, wandering around looking for an honest man."

"And you get paid?" Apache is smiling, and John K.

relaxes, because he's pulling his leg. The young man is heckling him, before he's even heard him say anything. That has to be a first.

"Not always. Not enough, for sure."

"But you're not famous."

"Not really. No."

"And I'll bet you're not very funny, either."

John K. looks away from the TV that he's not really watching anyhow, to see Apache wink at him. He is surprised he's not defensive about the crack.

"No. There was a time I was. That is, I think I used to be, but...,"

"Good. I like you more, all busted and honest." The young man gets up and walks to the bar to order a couple more very bad beers.

"He has a Mercedes Benz diesel – you know he drives that Nazi-mobile at senile-five miles per hour to the corner Wa Wa at seven-thirty in the fucking AM in khakis, a pit-stained wife-beater and penny-loafers to get half-and-half for his morning coffee, yelling out the window at the morning traffic honking at him to move for god's sake just a little bit faster, like it's only out there just to piss him off. He is so cheap, he has a 'no farms, no food' bumper sticker over a spot where a kid keyed his car for taking two spots in the grocery store parking lot. No farms, no food? I think you've missed the point. Shit, we're going to eat you, you miserable fat fuck, when all the farms go tits-up. I've already claimed dibs on one of your thighs in Apocalypse Bingo, slow-rotisseried, for me and my wife and her mom and dad, my children. And my cousin Fred and his girlfriend. And their dog, Astro...."

◆◆◆

45

# 5

It would seem that nobody's coming. The soggy boondoggle king of all interview assignments. They can't have cancelled the damned thing, could they? The worst part, Joan thinks, is that her backside is damp, from water running down her neck to her back, to her trousers and down to her butt-crack and so on. The best part, if there is a best part, is that she knows what time the damned thing is supposed to start, and that time is now, and if it's on, there's no one out here, so…. the man with the mustache was right – everyone came in a different way. After all, who uses front doors anymore? She would like to just drop the microphone on the sidewalk and stomp off, but the mic isn't hers and it's expensive. More valuable than she is to the station, probably.

"What do you want to do?" Antwerp asks, as he wipes the camera again with the damp chamois.

"Find that other door?" Her friend grins approval and she relinquishes the mic to him for safety and they run, don't walk, to Park Avenue Tower. Of course, that damned thing has to be closed – it's late. Joan crosses her fingers, pushes the heavy revolving door and it moves – presto! They're in, soggy sneaks squeaking on the floor. Here's an information desk, but there's no one at the information desk. Snoop around time.

But there's nothing here that leads there. Out the Fifty-sixth

Street entrance they sprint, sort of, and give that side of things a few minutes of time wasted. Mope back inside.

They slide against the slick wall to squat on the floor of the semi-dark lobby. Joan is bummed. Wet and bummed. Wet-bummed and bummed.

"We're not giving up, are we?" asks Antwerp. He likes this sort of stuff, working but not working. Getting paid to be a bit silly. He hopes Joan will maybe like hanging out with him when they are back at the station. She's smart, nice, funny. Or they can have dinner together sometime. Of course, not everything in the world turns out the way you want it to. Still…

It would seem, Joan the problem-solver thinks, there's no other way in. Not for regular people. Only for assassins. Or cat burglars. Or, what? Second storey men?

"Holy shit," she hisses.

"What?"

"The mustache said second-storey man. You think…?"

"Upstairs?" says Antwerp. "Where's an elevator?"

The door slides open and they are in a hallway, turned around a little bit, but it only takes a moment and they find the corridor that leads to the rear entrance of the Erdmann house. A heavy, carved oak door.

"Well I'll be damned," Joan mutters, and takes back the microphone from Antwerp and hangs it in her coat pocket. Now for some serious bullshit. She pulls off her Kangol again and with her free hand tries to fix her hair, but that's simply a bridge too far.

Of course there must be some kind of security for this entrance, this speakeasy style wooden door with a little spyhole. A bouncer, an entire herd of bouncers, or a modern electronic

47

badge device for members only. But there's not. The door tugs right open as well. And right inside is that production team member – the club's complete asshole. His name is Allen on his hello-sticky and he has ditched the clipboard with the scribbled complaints that no one is going to look at, and has a little table set-up about the size of something for two people to play a few hands of rummy, and two chairs, because if you're going to sit somewhere like this, well of course you want people to come and sit down and chat with you. Which Joan, reading the room perfectly, does.

"Hi, I'm Joan."

"Allen."

"Hey, Allen." She holds out the microphone, equal parts inviting and threatening. "We're one of the crews working on the Carroll O'Connor documentary? I was instructed to get the release form signed by a senior employee before we roll film inside the building. So, that would be you…Allen?" She peers at his nametag as if she was already too bored to remember him telling it to her four seconds ago.

Now it is Antwerp who bites his cheek to keep from smiling. *Ooh, you're such a fibber*. In the spirit of things, he pulls out a crumpled release form, slightly soggy because he's also used it to wipe moisture from the camera lens. He wishes he hadn't, but there you are, and he slaps it down on the little table as if this is standard operating procedure. Maybe it even is, but he has no idea.

Allen is not having the best night. A predictable number of complaints about food, facilities, the inability to find a private space to do hard drugs, the lack of ridiculously expensive single-malt scotch brands, hand-distilled tequilas and obscure micro-brews, and earlier there was someone requesting a fresh pair of Calvin Klein boxer-briefs, waist size 42. He didn't want to know why, but called Macy's anyhow, where the person who answered the phone laughed and laughed and hung up. And he's hungry – because far be it for the Club to give him a plate of their cruddy dinner.

"Documentary?"

"It's called Carroll O'Connor, From His Bunker." Joan is proud of herself for thinking on her feet. "PBS stuff, despite the silly pun." That last she feels a bit ashamed of, but there's no going back now.

Allen sits there, looking at the damp piece of paper on his table. How much does he give a shit that this is just a prank, something dumb for which no one will care, or if they do, will come back to bite him on the ass? Perhaps if they gave him something important to do, or paid him the slightest bit of atten-tion or an appropriate salary? It's a roiling cascade of complex questions, and his head has been hurting a little bit for about a half-hour, so he doesn't even bother to answer. He sighs.

"Is he here, yet?" Joan asks.

"He?"

"Mr. O'Connor."

"Of course."

"You've seen him?"

"Yes," Allen replies, as if it is no big deal. "He's in the Green room." Maybe he is. Allen has no idea.

"Can you take us there?" Joan asks, with as much of the same tone of boredom she can muster. "Or point the way?"

"Oh, no. You see I have to work this table." And as soon as it comes out of his mouth, Allen knows it's a mistake, because there is nothing here but the two chairs, the table, his sharpied nametag, the wet piece of paper, Joan and Antwerp.

"I see. The table," Joan withers. "Nice."

And they play the silent game together. Allen looks at Joan. Joan at Allen. The first one to flinch will lose. Joan knows this game. It's Thanksgiving with her family and every relationship she's ever been in. She will sit here until doomsday, or the cops arrive and carry her off.

"Aren't you going to interview me?" he finally asks.

"Why?" Joan retorts, playing with the microphone. "You're not one of the roasters, are you? Practically famous?"

"No," says Allen, semi-rebuffed. He is just playing her little game, it has backfired, so he chooses a new tack. He actually wants someone to talk to. "But I've worked here at the Friars for a good while. I did want to be a comic, when I was younger, but working here I know now what a mistake that is."

"Yeah?" says Joan. "How is it a mistake?" She taps her foot which she hopes will be code enough for Antwerp to turn on the damned camera.

"It should come as no surprise, but they're all crazy, one way or another. I know, I know – you're not supposed to say people are crazy, but stand-up is like…a virus they caught at some point that they share with each other, and the different variants feed on each other and it makes them all crazier."

Antwerp lifts his camera up to his hip and begins recording, turns on Joan's mic. She's holding it still, and it's picking up the man's words clearly enough. They're on the same page. You just never know, he thinks, when something is going to be worth capturing.

"Do you mean, like, they push each other?" Joan asks softly, not wanting to step on his words, or derail the ideas in his head with her own.

"Yes. Like children. No, correction: more like teenaged

boys. You put a couple of them in the same place and they will mostly ignore each other. Add a third one and then it's one-upsmanship time. They pack, like wolves on the hunt for utter insanity. Who can light the longest fart. Who's been the hungriest, the thirstiest, hurt the most gerbils, gasped the most coke up their nostrils. The bits get grittier, more invasive.

"There's an old, greasy sheet of paper on the Green room wall, with initials on it, that represents people, the comics, along with numbers. It gets updated, too, with new initials. I swear, it's been up there since the '80s, probably earlier. Way before my time. It's now covered with a sheet of acrylic, to keep it protected. They use it to place bets on who will die next. The numbers after the initials are the current odds, and the betting is done pari-mutuel style. And someone - a bunch of someones but I don't know who – keep the money and track the betting. Making the payouts as someone passes. Maybe it was always like this, I don't know. I keep waiting for the dates of death to show up on the paper, written in ink. And they think it's funny. Deeply, darkly funny.

"Like maybe there isn't something called too far. I don't know about that. But here's the thing; there's another piece of paper tacked up there, newer than the initials list. This one is a scribbled list of ways to die. It's a lot longer list, with way more different handwriting, with stapled additions on cocktail napkins and scraps of old bar receipts and so on. You can't really keep track of every idea, but that's the point. Like it's not the work of one person, but a group thing, a piece of performance art. A suggestion box for kicking the bucket. I can imagine whenever someone is in the green room, they check on their own standings, and tweak their own plans for taking a dirt nap."

Joan blinks at this. Dirt nap – she hasn't heard that one

before. It's very good. Terrible. Awful. Quite something.

"I mean, what other profession does this?" Allen shakes his head. "Cops? Those guys who paint the Golden Gate Bridge? Navy SEALs? I doubt it. I think only stand-up would find this…grim enough to be entertaining."

"I never really thought of telling jokes as a profession," Joan says, almost to herself. Now it is Allen's turn to be surprised.

"…No?" His eyebrows crumple into a frown. "Why not?"

"I guess it always seemed more like an affliction than a profession." Joan smiles at the seeming profundity of her words.

"That's what I'm saying!" Allen barks a laugh, like he's clearing his throat. His laughter, analyzed from this one out-burst, sounds rusty. Something he doesn't do often. "Comedy is a disease. An allergy. I'll buy that."

A rumble from further within the old house, a mix of human voices and applause. Strange how crowd approval is similar to thunder, or what Antwerp thinks a distant earthquake must sound like. He taps his foot softly and when Joan looks over, pulls his finger across his neck in the sign for cut. She smiles and nods. It is completely silly – she should be deciding when the camera rolls or doesn't, but it doesn't seem to trouble Allen. She stands and hands the microphone to Antwerp.

'Twerp doesn't turn off the camera, but lowers it to his hip, still rolling. You never know, he thinks. He ups the recording power of the microphone with his thumb and holds it out like a lollypop.

"Thank you for that," Joan says to the young man at the table. "There's some good footage there, I think." She taps the release form and Allen pulls the silver Mark Cross pen from his jacket pocket and signs the bottom with a flourish that almost tears the paper.

"Allen!" They all turn. It sounds like an old woman. Like a boy's mom yelling for him to stop playing in the muddy back yard.

"Oh, shit. The Dean of Friars," Allen mutters. "Yes sir!"

Then they have to wait while the man walks down the hall, his shoes clip-clop clapping on the linoleum. For any student of comedic timing, this takes longer than it should. Antwerp turns his body to aim the camera in that direction.

"Who are these people, Allen?" The Dean puts his hands on his hips. It is not much of a threatening look. Joan bites back her smile.

"Television, sir."

"Are they supposed to be here?"

"I couldn't say for certain, sir."

"May I help you?" the Dean says, turning theatrically to face Joan. She holds her seat. Getting away with something is largely a matter of seeming like you belong. Relaxing when everyone is uptight. Countering threat with offhand confidence. Ignoring your very messy hair. The Dean of Friars is short, elderly, wearing an old fashioned, thin-lapeled tuxedo that fits well, she supposes, but still doesn't flatter him. Maybe nothing can. His hair is too long over his large ears and his jowls are so loose they don't disappear when he smiles, like he's doing now. It is not a real smile, anyhow. The oxfords on his feet are good, though, and well-polished. Isn't that one measure of a person, however small? Mostly, Joan decides, he looks like someone who owns a basset hound and likes talking on the phone with his feet on the desk.

"We're here for the documentary." She tosses the same bullshit over the wall as before. May it not come back.

53

"What documentary?" The Dean of Friars has a strange, warbly voice up close, too. It must be part of his thing, his schtick.

Joan looks him in the eye, represses a sudden urge to fix her hair, and doesn't think the lie about Carrol O'Connor will work again, not with the boss of the whole roast mess. She has a nanosecond to consider her response, not nearly enough time, and blurts out something different. And that's when some sort of magic happens. A germ of an alternative idea. She gives Allen an instant of eye-contact and throws the pitch.

"John K. You know, his career, what it's like putting yourself out there, a view from the inside, the ups and downs and back-ups again of being a comic. Pretty normal stuff, only we're also approaching it all through the eyes of his loved ones."

She can see that the Dean of Friars is a heartbeat away from tossing them out. Oh, not himself, of course – he couldn't toss both of them out. Could toss the microphone, probably, but that's it. But it would be quite the ruckus.

"We're here with his father, to get a little live A-reel footage with his POV at the roast." She uses the acronym POV as if everyone knows precisely what she means. Maybe they do, maybe they don't. Who cares? It sounds technical enough.

The Dean of Friars feels his eyes go wide. Oh. Well. John K. and his father. That makes sense. Maybe there's something juicy going on here that he needs to be aware of. He wonders if there's time before the actual roast.

"Well, you can't record this show. Not for television," says the Dean of Friars, giving Allen another look of deep dissatisfaction for making him come out here and do his job for him.

"Oh," Joan says, amazed at the luck she has manufactured out of whole cloth. "We have no intention of doing this for broadcast television. We just work for the _____ network. This is a project sponsored by them. It will probably end up on PBS or a direct-to-video piece. Things usually work out like that."

"Hmm," says the Dean. The patter the young woman is giving him is starting to be confusing. She is answering questions he's not asking. Is she lying? He would like very much to be A-reel footage.

"So, do we need to buy a ticket or something?" Joan asks. If the man says yes, that will be a problem, as she hasn't got her credit card with her, and suspects that between Anterp and herself, they've enough money to buy one Starbucks Frappuccino. Maybe a Vente, maybe not. There is a cheer and rolling laughter from within the building and the Dean turns his head, irritated that he is missing something.

"Handle this, Allen," the Dean attempts to growl, but it comes out a warble. Then he clippity-clops back down the hallway. They all wait until the sound recedes to nothing.

"Well, Allen?" says Joan, with a smile. We're all in this together. "Is there a ticket we can purchase?"

"No," Allen replies. He's sort of shaking his head, at the goofiness of the situation he's currently in, at the stupidity of his job, at what an asswipe the Dean of Friars is.

"Good, because we haven't got any money. Do you think they're still serving dinner?" Joan pushes the envelope, hard.

"Probably not, but certainly there's still something in the kitchen."

"You're hungry aren't you?" She looks at both Antwerp and Allen with eyebrows raised. "Let's get a bite to eat and see if we can't film something. Something funny." She gets up from her chair, and Allen finds that he just doesn't give a shit what anyone else says. Maybe this night won't completely suck after all.

"We should skip the trout," he says and leads the way to the kitchen.

# 6

John K pulls slowly away from Apache for only a moment. He's not handsome, not really. It's something else. What's wrong with him? What's wrong with me that I'm here? John K. is so used to finding fault in everything that the question bounces back and forth like this, over and over. Knock it off! he shouts silently at himself.

"What is it?" Apache asks.

"You were supposed to tell me what time it is."

The messenger looks at his own wristwatch.

"It's I don't give a damn thirty," he says and kisses John K. again.

"I have to leave," John K. says.

"But that's not what you were thinking, is it?"

"Yes. No. I was thinking how I'm not much on romance."

"No, you weren't. Nobody thinks those words." Apache chuckles.

"Maybe not. Come with me?"

"Me? Not a chance. My shoes are wet."

"It doesn't matter."

"Sure it does. Wet shoes always matter. Anyway, I have to head downtown and clock out. Then get some sleep. And something to eat."

"There's food where I'm going."

"Anything good?"

"Oh, god, no. It'll be awful."

"That bad, huh? Then why did you mention it?" Apache tilts his head quizzically.

"I don't know. Lack of self-control, maybe." John K. leans forward and steals another sweet, scratchy kiss.

"Apparently, in our modern society, we're not allowed to make fun of you for being fat. I don't understand this. I mean, I can call you an idiot, I can say you're a horrible human being, as lacking in talent as an empty grocery bag, but I can't call you fatso. It is your fault you're fat, you Wonderbread eating asshole. You sausage and gravy swilling monster. But, I get it, I really do. You can't be blamed for your shape anymore. OK, then. I'll be sensitive. Can I still call you an asshole? A gigantic asshole? We can still say that, right? Let me check with our judges, those complete retards, and get a decision on the asshole situation. Wait. I can't say retard? Are you fucking kidding me? What? I can't say kid?"

Another long moment. They just sit with their arms over each other's shoulders, and their foreheads touching, each breathing the other in like pure oxygen.

"I do have to go," John K. says, finally. "I'm late."

"Better late than dead," the younger man says. "Go. Do good."

"Do good? You obviously haven't been listening," John K resorts to his persona, but Apache pats him on the arm.

"Yes, I have. Do good."

John K. smiles, stands up from the metal café stool. No one he can remember has ever said that to him. Does the man mean do well, in which case he will do the best he can, or actually do good – acts of value – an aspect of existence he has so rarely considered that it is eye-openingly fresh to him. How can he do good? He's never done good before. It will be more than a bit tricky.

"I'm going to do my five. It's pretty ugly. Not very tight." Suddenly it feels important that he tell the truth to the young man. Strangely so.

"Yes. I understand."

"If I do this, maybe I get to keep doing this. That's kind of a fucked-up reason, but it's all I have. I can leave right after."

Apache laughs at the irony.

"No," he whispers. "You stay and be part of the thing."

"So how will I find you again?" John K. asks. It is so open a question and so unlike him that he actually feels shivers down his spine. Like the words fell out of his mouth, unbidden. Un-bitten.

"Do you want to find me again?"

"I think I do."

"And I want to be found. Alright. Then it will happen."

Apache unlocks and shoulders his bike and walks over, deft-ly negotiates the door and disappears. John is fascinated by how much he wishes he had been kissed goodbye. He stands.

It has stopped raining outside. It's nice. Whatever weather pattern it was that was slowly pushing through the city has just decided to be done. Funny how summer ends at Labor Day, packs up and just vamooses. John K. ambles across 55th at the light, and down to the little house with three maroon awnings, made charcoal gray by the distant streetlamps. Shit, he thinks and pushes open the door. Let's hear it for The Late John K.

"...he used to show up for work on Mondays and someone on the production crew would announce 'this is going to get ugly,' and then make-up would hog-tie him to his chair."

There's a small serving table with a bench behind it near the kitchen door, with a very large, droopy-leafed, green potted plant attempting to block it from view. It works. Mostly. They take possession of it, hip to hip, laden with plates, forks, napkins and drinks. Antwerp thinks the plant's a fake, the sort of painted-silk thing that they use in movies about jungles. It has dust on the leaves, he explains to Joan, who is tempted to reach out and touch it to be sure. No, Allen tells her, don't. It's real. And it also blocks them from view, so there's that. Antwerp has asked Allen if he may set his camera up, hiding it in the plant, and record what they can. Allen assures him that it is quite possible he could give less of a shit what happens now, however he isn't sure that it's probable. Antwerp arranges the microphone as well, perching it in the crotch of a branch. While it is not a shame that they don't have better seats, it would have been nice to have brought more suitable equipment, some kind of shotgun mic more appropriate for directional audio capture. They're behind and to the left of the riser, so what they see won't be good video, but they will have the only recording of the event, for whatever that's worth. And they have only slightly overcooked baked garlic chicken and oven-browned potatoes, with wilted spinach and capers. Being very hungry makes this food particularly yummy. Sitting behind a bush makes it silly, but still fun.

"I think we need some wine." Allen says to no one. He is hip-deep in the spirit of self-destructiveness that one gets when one imagines imminent unemployment. Or when one is kidnapped by pirates.

"Yes, we do," says Joan, feeling playful and useless.

"Shall I fetch some?"

"Please. Do it," Joan insists, sounding a lot like that kid who tells the others to shoplift candy, while not putting anything in their own pocket. She's sipping a glass of watery vodka rocks that she pilfered from a sympathetic kitchen staffer. Surely there is more wine. There is always more wine. Allen pushes an argumentative plastic-esque fern frond out of his way and steps back into the noisy kitchen.

"You may not have known this, but back when he was young and skinny and had hair and talent, he was one of the original Beatles. He would sit in the loo with an Ampex reel-to-reel tape machine and record his farts. Sort of a Pete Second-Best. A Ringo Fallen-Starr or John Lemon. He was the dung Beatle. He's grown now. You can groan now, too."

The Old Man thinks he wants an after-dinner scotch. Correction; another. He's already had his one, a self-imposed limit because he knows it will stove him up even worse than he already is. He sits back and rubs his ample belly through the fake vest of his tux. His gut is gurgling after having consumed some of his dinner, although he is quite certain that his shit is still just adhering to his intestinal walls like metamorphic layers of stone that will eventually be some geologist's mystery, a calcified, coprolithic enigma in the ground of what was once a Manhattan landmark, long forgotten. He also knows he is not really paying attention to the roast. What he's hearing is Brand X insult humor, the low-grade crush-and-run bullshit that is used to pave roads to comedic ruin. What is there new to say about

59

how we see the human condition in others?  Are you ugly, stupid, misshapen, wrong-headed, suffering with poor judgment, not suffering with it at all, but blissfully wallowing in your idiocy?  Maybe he really is too old for this kind of stuff.  He could always just leave, get up from his seat, exit the room, grab his coat and hat and have Guy or Bud or Mac hail him a cab.  No he can't - someone will see, his retreat will be noticed.  That would become the thing.  He'll hear about it.  He doesn't want to hear about anything.

He misses the old days, before there were rules like…at all. Smoke up, my friend.  All the drinks you want.  Tell me a joke! Just be funny – we don't give a damn how you make us laugh. Take out your balls and drag them through the cold-cuts.  Now people get offended.  They laugh, are caught in the act of laughing, and oh, now they're offended.

"She told me that you and she had an affair, albeit brief, and reported that you weren't terrible in the sack, which is a participation trophy if ever I heard one.  That you are trapped in the dictionary between incompetence and incontinence.  You blamed your mediocrity on everything under the sun other than your own ineptitude.  She did say, however, you gave her multiple sarcasms.  As for me, I find it difficult to believe that anyone would fuck you.  I find it equally, or close enough to equally to qualify, believable that if you were told to do so you would go fuck yourself.  So, a toss-up question.  Could you please eat shit and die?"

He gives a little grunt of a laugh at the cosmos, just one. Then he slowly pushes back his chair, clenches his buttocks as tightly as he is able so he doesn't break audible wind, and buttons his jacket – one, two.  Just going to the head, he tells himself. Give it the old college try. The only way there without being noticed is through the kitchen, or at least into the kitchen then through that madhouse labyrinth to the back door and the hell out of here. He'll forego fetching his raincoat and hat.

But he walks right into the table. Of course he does. John K.'s father's table. He is alone, thank any gods that actually still exist, but there's no quick escape. He stands there two beats too long and now has to acknowledge him. Fuck. Fuckity-fuck.

"Good to see you again." The mustache twitches its bristles in direct counterpoint to the pleasantry. So very not true.

"Well. Hello," says the Old Man. He doesn't hold out his hand for shaking. The mustache doesn't seem to notice or care.

"How are things by you?" asks the mustache, pushing the pleasantries out of his mouth with a broom. "You're up to-night?"

"Probably." The answer is cryptic, but unintentionally. The Old Man doesn't want to talk about work, not with the mustache. And for all he can tell, it was poorly hidden snark about being awake this late, not going up to the microphone to speak. Shit, you dinosaur, you're about as old as I am. "You here for the trout almondine?"

"Absolutely," says the mustache. "I'm a big fan of dead fish. A treat for the senses. No. The kid is up. I hope."

"Ha. Excellent," says the Old Man, surprised by the revelation, and therefore somewhat incoherent. Was John K. even here? He'd been a wunderkind, back at some point. Then a meltdown. Predictable. Or is it inevitable? One implies the other, of course.

"We'll see." The mustache offers the Old Man the chair across from him. The Old Man sighs and sits. Well, he wasn't going to crap anyway.

61

"If I say he's old, and you shout, 'how old?!', bouncers are going to come around the room and take away your drink tickets. Even the ones you stole. You just have to trust me, he's very old. Really ancient. Like he was one of the guys who sold Brutus the knife to stab Julius Caesar. There, you got your history lesson for the day. And cheap. So cheap he made Brutus pay extra for sharpening the dagger. Brutus made him drop trou' to prove he wasn't Jewish. Yeah. Waiter! I'm going to need another drink myself before I go into what he looks like with his pants down."

The mustache sips a short glass of brown liquor. A rye old-fashioned, the Old Man guesses. Too sweet for him to ever have learned to enjoy.

"What was the name of that guy?" he asks.

"Which guy?" says the Old Man.

"The one who wouldn't admit that he stole punchlines."

"You mean the one who liked the Yankees? Wore the warm-up jacket?"

"No, not the one who liked the Yankees. That guy was a putz. The other guy who wasn't a putz."

"Shit. They were all putzes. Why? He's not here, is he? Someone must have wheeled him in. God, he would have to be…" The Old Man likes picking on other old people frailer than he. It's one of the few distinctly schadenfreude joys of being old.

"No he's not here. He's dead," says the mustache, frowning at the Old Man. "He's been dead for a few years. Not my point."

"OK. Really? Dead. I'll be damned. Fucking putz. What is your point?" The Old Man is actually surprised, and makes a note to himself to regret having joked about wheeling him in. Of course people do keep dying. It's what we do. Our best thing. He sits back in the chair, massaging his uncomfortable belly through the tuxedo vest like he's rubbing Buddha for good luck.

"The reason he wouldn't admit he stole anything is that he took the punchlines and made them better jokes."

"No he didn't…" the Old Man starts, but the mustache cuts him off with a curt and dismissive wave of his hand.

"Oh, come on. He stole them and made them better, and we all got pissed off and ganged up on him. They were just OK when we did them, but he made them crisp and fresh and funny and no one out there beyond the lights cared that they might have heard them before, on some other stage out of some other mouth. Why isn't that the thing? Instead, we cut him off from the pack. Blackballed him because he was a thief. We hated him for it. And not because he was better than us, which was the truth. Because that's what we do. We lie to ourselves. Lie to ourselves that we have something worth saying." The mustache hunches his shoulders and looks around, as if he's aware that someone might be listening to his rant. Actually, he's looking for someone to get him another rye old-fashioned.

"What do you do with a thief, then? Let him keep stealing?" The Old Man recalls that one joke, the one about Jesus and Judas' thirty pieces of silver. Or was it the thirty pieces of silver the Midianites sold Joseph for? OK, maybe he couldn't recall that joke.

"I don't know," the mustache says. "I really don't. Maybe you open the fucking door and let him in and tell him to take whatever he wants. Because he's gonna do something great with it."

The Old Man shakes his head, because it's too much for

63

right now. His heart isn't really in the argument. He feels like they're two Talmudic scholars shaking their fingers at each other, each certain that their pointed perspective is the right one and anything else is blasphemy. But the mustache might be right. It's a hell of a thing trying to make people laugh. You spit between your fingers and walk around stepladders and stop dating women with big feet because you don't want to mess with the thing, and things go wrong anyway or they go too well and your funny sloughs off like a snake's skin. Still, the joke thief is dead. How do you like that shit? Long live the king.

"All seriousness: he has the attitude of someone who desperately wants the moniker 'Bulldog,' so everyone will think he won't give up, won't give an inch. Fair enough, he has the body of someone who never backs up, because they're unable to see in their rear-view mirror. Trust me, buddy, you don't want to see your rear view. It's a horror show."

No one notices the mustache, so no one comes to take the empty glass. The two elderly gentlemen sit and watch the show.

# 7

In the back of the room, John K. stands with his hands in his pockets. From here he can see the hallway to the stairs leading down to the front entrance. Which is also an exit. He can also view the dais, with its microphone'd oak podium. The roasters sit mostly facing outward, blue-white tablecloths draped over church-picnic tables. The backs of heads of the audience members, flickering little lamps on the tables, drinking and eating, laughing, ignoring the show or paying too much attention. It's like a gangster movie, maybe, or an American Legion annual dinner to commemorate those who go before us.

He tried going to the Blue room, but it was no good. Lines of coke are no good. Idiots sitting on molded plastic chairs with their pants around their ankles getting head is probably no good. Money being transferred from one hand to another for insidious reasons unknown is rarely good. So he pretended he forgot something. Said "Oh, shit, that's right,' and snapped his finger dramatically, as if anyone within the Blue room gave a crap about what anyone else on Earth was doing or choosing not to do. Mostly, however, he found that he was talking to himself, a reminder that he's at about a quarter-to-midnight on the clock that says his fairy godmother is going to pull the plug in the tub and wash him down the drain, not to belabor multiple metaphors. Turn around, buddy boy. Go.

He's not alone. A small crowd of the dispossessed, misplaced folks who are hangers-on, the lowest, newest members, the plus ones, the people not invited but who still find a way to be places. The oldest tuxedos, scuffed at the elbows and knees, the most out of style. We poor, we tragically unhip.

"Hey, I know you," a pretty young woman with long brunette hair in Manhattan standard LBD and too-tall heels leans towards him and murmurs in his ear. Her breath is a battle between orange tic-tac and Virginia Slims.

"No, you probably have me mistaken."

"Do you got a light?" She ignores what he says. She has a bent smoke between her fingers.

"I'm sorry, I don't." He's still wearing his damp horseman's duster coat, and appears very much out of place, and is amused at how much he doesn't really care, and wonders if this is a new position for him, or just a temporary point of view. An anomaly, so to speak.

"Are you waiting for a table, too?" she asks. John K. looks at her quizzically. Her eyes are swollen, like she's been dabbing tears from them carefully, with a hanky or tissue, so as not to foul her make-up. Something's gone wrong. Oh, boy.

"No. Are you?"

"Yes." She accidentally leans against him for just a moment, failing the balancing act on her skyscraper shoes.

"Sorry," she says. He shrugs a no big deal.

"Where are you from?"

"Jersey," she replies. John K. bites back low hanging fruit about New Jersey.

"Did someone tell you that they were getting you a table?"

"Of course," says the pretty woman, carefully straightening and putting away her cigarette in a pack that takes up most of the space in her little clutch.

"Um," says John K. "That's not how it works." He sees the Old Man sitting across from…the mustache. Holy crap. Well, he's here. John K. resists the temptation to close his eyes and blink them open, as if imagining a new result in which the mustached man is still in Boston or Bangor or Bangkok or anywhere but here.

"But, what do I do, then?" asks the pretty woman. John K. has an answer, another shitty snark of a response, but for the third time he denies the urge and listens for the cock's crow. For some reason that he senses he already knows but will need more time to verify, he swallows back his natural bile. She doesn't deserve anything he thinks he needs to dish out, he tells himself. So just put it down.

"It's OK," he turns to her. She's almost too young to be here, he decides, and takes her gently by the elbow. "What's your name?"

"Nicole."

"OK, Nicole. I'm John. Come with me. We'll sit at this table right over here." And he walks towards the two old gentlemen. It's a long, hard walk, but there have been a few of them tonight, so maybe he's getting better at it. Funny how that works.

"The part of the show that was bullshit to me was that Archie had a kid. Not just a kid but a girl child, and she had grown up into adulthood and hadn't poisoned anyone in her family in their sleep. Like herself. Her mother. Him.

67

"So, anyhow, this daughter, one Gloria by name, was a good character, a kind person, played well. Starts off as dim as a candle on the other side of a bombed-out cathedral, and grows brighter over time. Her dresses were short of material, but not her part. And you complained to the writers about this, and they told you if you wore the dress, you'd get the jokes. Thank all of the gods you decided to not be funny."

"Holy shit," mutters the Old Man, loud enough for John and the girl to hear.

"Nice mouth," the mustache growls. He stands up from his chair.

"Nicole, I know these two guys," John says. "They're mean and old, and ugly and have terrible table manners, but they're harmless enough that you should be able to get a drink and a plate of whatever they're serving for supper and probably even a light for your cigarette. If they try to touch you, stab them with your fork. Guys, this is Nicole. I'll be checking back with her to see how well you've behaved."

"Hello, John," the mustache says.

"Hiya, Pop," John K. replies. "Nicole, believe it or not, this is my dad. We were standing over there, and Nicole got stood up or something, and she's hungry."

"Holy shit," says the Old Man again. "I mean, pardon my French. Hello. Please, have a seat." He does grab the attention of one of the rent-a-penguins and orders a bottle of white and the chicken plate. And a rye old-fashioned for the mustache. Cracks open his wallet and actually hands the waiter a Jackson so he'll hurry. His stomach doesn't hurt anymore. This girl is so young. Or he's so damned old. The very idea takes his breath away.

"When are you up?" asks the mustache, when everyone is sitting again.

"I don't know. Soon."

The girl, Nicole, turns to him.

"Are you going to talk?" Did she say talk? Oh, my god, he thinks. New Jersey...

"Maybe," John K. says. "When they say my name. Or if they do."

"I knew you were famous," she says. He smiles. Famous. It's a generous term.

"How's your stuff?" asks the Old Man. It's a strange question, John K. thinks, like asking a child if they're ready for an exam. But for it to come from this fellow is quite something, another detail of the evening he will have to save for now and analyze later, when there is an opportunity to roll everything around in his head and make sense of it.

"Not bad...,"

"...but not good." the mustache finishes the old chestnut. "Well...." But whatever he thinks he was going to say drifts away, as it sometimes does.

"Yeah," says John K. "Well."

"I loved your work in 'Rambo, First Blood.' What? Oh, that wasn't you? Brian Dennehy? Ah-ha. So how about 'Deliverance'? You were terrific rowing a boat and getting bent over by the rednecks. Still not you? Oh, well, it was Texas sheriff someone or Major-General Somebody or Blah-blah the bus driver. No? Jeez, all you lumpy white old bastards look alike. Eventually."

So Joan is drunk. In her defense, she doesn't mean to be. She and Antwerp and Allen have eaten their dinners like starving orphans, sneaked back for seconds, and broken into a second bottle of pilfered wine. One of the stewards in the kitchen has also brought them some pretty good crème brulee, served chilled in tartlet cups, the sugary covering well-caramel'd. No one else, the steward told them, got crème brulee. There simply wasn't enough to go around. Joan has even interviewed the steward, because why not? His name is Rupert Dominguez, or maybe something different, she cannot ask him a third time. They've insisted that he sit with them and tell his story. He's from a small town in Nicaragua, but has lived in Paterson, New Jersey for a half dozen years, working in the catering trade. He wants to go to school, become something completely different, but he's not sure what. The others – Allen, Antwerp and Joan – listen politely yet intoxicated and then try to dissuade Rupert from making rash education decisions.

"You don't like what you do?" Rupert asks, puzzled.

"God, no," says Allen explosively, then ducking his head as if someone behind him might hear this treason. There is no one behind him but the plaster and paint of the wall. "It's the worst job ever."

Joan taps Allen on the arm and shakes her head slowly and dramatically.

"Oh, Allen, it's not a terrible job. It's just bad. Annoying. You see, Rupert, here in New York there are people doing what they want to do for lots of money, people doing what they don't enjoy for lots of money. Mostly these folks are pretty pleased. Then there are people doing what they don't want to do for a little money. They're probably not happy, but they're divided into two more groups, those who don't have a choice and keep doing the job well, and there are those who have a choice. Some of them have a plan to try and do something else. They're people like you. You will move on from this. Then there are people like Allen, and me. Maybe even Antwerp here. We will continue to do the thing we don't like very much because we can't make ourselves move on. We're…adverse to change."

"Averse." Antwerp says. Joan gives her friend a puzzled look.

"That's what I said. A verse."

"Sure. OK."

"I can move on," says Allen, slowly getting up from his seat. "Does anyone want anything from the kitchen?"

"I can get it for you," says Rupert, standing. Allen takes off his tuxedo jacket and pulls on the sleeve of Rupert's white smock.

"Switch." So the two men change coats and Rupert sits back down and nibbles some cold potatoes with his fingers while Allen goes forth from behind the ferny forest to hunt for bigger and better game.

"I'm actually afraid to pick on him, even in so-called fun, because I'm concerned that, like the pitbull he resembles, he'll turn on me and take a chunk out of my leg. He's one of those friendly looking dogs, a crazy-grandpa type that has a wooden box of old moss-covered pine-apple grenades that he snuck out of Korea during the war and hides in a hole he dug in the basement of his suburban home, next to the gas water heater. Like, what could possibly go wrong?"

It's nice to feel nervous. Well, not nice, but refreshing. It's good to give a shit about what's coming. May be coming. He's still not certain that he will be handed the mic, called up to the podium and allowed to roll. Yet, even that is a welcome feeling.

John K. is watching the Old Man chattering away with Nicole, who is blithely adapting to her evening; nodding and smiling, sipping and laughing, chewing and blotting her lips with

71

a linen napkin. He wonders who she was really supposed to be with, which complete imbecile dumped her at the door. Or did she just come up to the front door, give it a shove, and bluff her way to here and now? That is just as fascinating a possibility.

The noise of the show is New York normal. Anyone who lives here knows, there is background and it never ends. Sirens. Car horns. Jets overhead. Telephones ringing. Everything else in-between. So you learn to find your way through the clutter, your ears doing something like a pedestrian dance along Madison Avenue at day's end, working around the noise to what you want to hear.

"You know him?" asks the mustache quietly, pointing his thumb over his shoulder at the show. The current comic's bit is slow, carefully staged.

John K. listens to the guy at the podium. Good ol' Jimmy. Yeah. They're peers, if there's such a thing in the business. Climbed up through the same ratholes back in the days when clubs with names like Funhouse and Insane Asylum were popping up in every city. Everyone was on the road, sharing early morning deli, splitting the cost of a dime bag. All for one and one for all, sort of.

"Yeah," he says. "He's OK."

"It's stale."

"It's all stale, Pop." It feels a little weird to call his father Pop, but he does it anyway, which means that it must be an old habit, an ancient rune chipped in the archeology of his skull. It also is strange to be giving him his opinion on something. When did it ever count for anything?

"What happened, do you think?" asks the mustache. "When did everything go flat? Did we just get to the end of the book, and now we have to close it and open again at the beginning?"

John K. gives his father a look, just to make sure that he's not pulling his leg.

"I don't know. I don't think so. I think it'll get better. It will get funny again." The words are true, but at least they're not fraught with world-weary sighs and frustrated curses. In his own ears he sounds like the pep-talking coach of a very bad team, maybe middle-school basketball, where everyone just keeps running up and down the court, hogging the ball or throwing it wildly out of bounds. "And it's a Monday. I cannot imagine why they picked a Monday night."

"What's happening tomorrow?" asks the mustache.

"I don't have a clue."

"No, I mean with you. Where you staying?"

"The Drake."

"Ah. So, you want to have breakfast?"

"Sure, Pop. Sure." It's done. A commitment. How do you like that? Then he'll head downtown. Maybe make another. Two in one day. Wouldn't that be something? So, breakfast it is.

"I hear you used to troll the studio commissary for...everything. Spare change. Stale croissant. Tall-haired, middle-aged housewives in high-waisted jeans and white pumps on long-weekend bus tours rolling down from Mill Valley. You were an indiscriminate predator, as likely to pinch a woman on the tits as steal the French fries off her plate as you strolled by, still in wardrobe. Always with that big Archie Bunker psycho-grimace smile, that seemed to constantly say 'shut up, you!' Fun fact: you held the world title of scary-funny-famous fat guy until that clown in Illinois that killed all the people."

Allen returns with something under his smock and a very sly, oh boy we're in trouble smile on his face. He sits, still

73

hiding whatever it is.

"What?" says Joan. Allen still grins like a Cheshire cat.

"What, what?" He opens the white smock. A bottle of Absinthe. It's green hour! Absinthe. The green monster even a Yankees' fan can love and fear in equal proportions.

"That's some serious shit," says Antwerp, swabbing out his coffee cup with the corner of the table-cloth and setting it down for a pour.

"Oh, bull," Joan elbows him playfully in the chest. "You've never had absinthe."

"Neither have you," is his noble defense.

"The French word absinthe," narrates Allen in a terrible Midlands BBC accent, "can refer either to the licorice-flavored alcoholic beverage, or less commonly, to the actual wormwood plant from which it originates. Absinthe is derived from the Latin absinthium, which in turn comes from the Greek ἀψίνθιον or apsínthion. It is also said that the word means 'undrinkable' in Greek. Ironically, it was, however, found consummately drinkable by Messrs. Ernest Hemingway, James Joyce, Lewis Carroll, Charles Baudelaire, Henri de Toulouse-Lautrec, Vincent van Gogh, Oscar Wilde, Marcel Proust, Edgar Allan Poe and Lord Byron. Good company if you insist on getting high, I suppose."

"So where'd you get it," Antwerp presses.

"I opened the liquor pantry," says Allen.

"But it is always locked, except when the Dean and the chief steward are there." Rupert says, eyes wide. "How did you?"

"Oh, the chief steward," says Allen. "I informed him that the Dean is getting lit at the moment and wants a little something to take the edge off. I also promised that if he was so interested, he could take for himself the twenty-six-year-old Macallan. He agreed to my negotiation."

"Holy shit," says Antwerp. "That's expensive."

"Yes, it is," Allen replies. "Your club dues at work."

"You're probably fired," Joan notes.

"No, no. I'm definitely fired," Allen says. "Hell, I'm probably under arrest." And he cracks the Absinthe bottle and pours a finger into each of his new friends' drinking receptacles. They stare at the stuff in their glasses and cups, as strangely green-tinted as an old-fashioned alien from outer space or the kooky not-at-all plastic plant they're ostensibly hiding behind.

"Isn't this just great? We're all gathered here at our secret club-house, laughing our fat drunk asses off because we're using dirty words and our moms can't stop us because they don't know we're out on a school night! Unless they pay our dues for us. Like, because we're broke. Thanks, Mom! No, I'm not ready to go to bed yet. Please! Five more minutes!"

Well more than five minutes have passed. Joan announces that she, too, is probably fired, so that Allen won't feel so bad about losing his job, should this event come to pass. Then she takes another slug of the green liquor, now a bit cloudy because they've added simple syrup they made at the table with tap water and sugar packets in a coffee-cup placed over one of the lamps. Why they'd placed it over the lamp no one would have been able to explain, other than it was one of them – possibly Rupert, whose credentials as an expert in drinking were rather suspect – remarked that you had to heat water to dissolve sugar into it.

'Twerp tugs the camera out of its hiding place and uses it to film them all taking absinthe shots, although the microphone remains in the bush, picking up the audio from the roast. He

75

wonders if the pictures correlate to the soundtrack. Allen's
smock – the one he'd traded Rupert for – is spattered with green
saliva so that he looks like he is either a wounded Vulcan from
Star Trek, or a frog-gigger, which apparently is a thing.

"What is a froggigger?" asks Allen, who can barely keep his
eyes open, much less assemble such a strange set of syllables, all
smashed into one word.

"The green ones. Little green. The ones like Kermit," Joan
explains, but the question she's answering hasn't been asked, so
no one knows why she's saying what she's saying. This makes
her laugh very hard and clap Antwerp on the shoulder and the
camera shakes violently, as if there has just been an earthquake
or something. It is serendipitous that at that moment the audience is applauding, so the shaking is fittingly…earthquaky. Then
Antwerp says hey, now, or something like that, which tickles
Joan even more so that she starts singing the lyrics to one song
and then slips into another that also famously contains those two
rather generic words. And sips her sickly-sweet drink.

In some social situations there are moments of singularity
when everyone is pleased with what is happening, pleased with
themselves, and apparently having such a good time to those outside that singularity that they create a gravitational pull as inex-
orable, if not quite as theoretically strong, as a black hole. Such
is the social situation behind the plant. But, just sometimes,
matter is flung away by the very force of the quantum-mechanics
/ down-the-drain spin of a black hole. Such as what happens to
Joan.

"I know that guy!" she shouts, and stands up. Reaches for
her drink and changes her mind. Tries to push back from the
table, but her seat is a bench that she is sharing with Allen and
Antwerp so it doesn't move and she sits down again against her

will with a bump and a burst of giggles. She tries again more carefully, sort of. Accidentally kicks each of them as she clambers off the bench. Grabs her glass and shoves dusty leaves out of her weaving way.

The mustache sees her coming in hard. He stands, bracing for impact.

Oh, geez. Here we go.

# 8

"Want some Absinthe?" Joan slides into the mustache's seat.

"Sure, sure," he takes the glass from her hand before she spills the nearly glowing alien green goop on everyone. Sets her glass safely on the table. Procures another chair and sits.

"Folks, this is…" he thinks for a moment. "Joan Jones of _____TV news. She's doing a piece about the roast." Then he introduces everyone at the table.

"Where is your television crew?" asks the Old Man, who is fascinated at the way the evening has mutated from a rather unpleasant task to a sort of party, to which he is pleased he was invited. A little drama, some new faces and stories, with just enough attention aimed his way.

"I don't…over there?" Joan points at the kitchen door. All heads turn.

No one knows what she sees that they don't. Everyone at her table is mostly hidden behind the great and powerful wizard of ferns.

"For god's sake, over there!" she shouts.

"Not everyone remembers what it was like back then. Well, some of you older depends-wearing bastards, but not everyone. A crossroads in American History. Or the crap part of it, anyhow. National Guardsmen found themselves somewhat frightened of college sophomores, and so perforated them with 5.56-millimeter ammunition. The duly elected President of the republic was concerned that the hard-working, vaguely sapient and yet steadily less relevant constituency of angry eighty-year-olds wouldn't show up to re-elect him, so it was suggested by one of his mongrel hounds that he send a small band of hand-picked clinical-retardates to jimmy open the doors and file cabinets of the offices of the other party's campaign. You know, just in case. It seemed a good idea at the time. And so, Archie Bunker. That classic bigoted loudmouth. Who can deny the cosmic, karmic, comic timing?"

Joan clutches the mustache by the hand, walking as if she is leading him to water, saying c'mere, c'mere like he's a puppy, and they stalk back across the room to the jungle hidden kitchen door table. The rest of the gang is there; quietly sipping, except for Rupert who has spilt his on the table and is wiping it around with a forefinger like a Pollock painting and then tasting the results.

"Guys, this is…" Joan begins with a flourish and then wobbles on her flats. "Shit. I don't even know your name."

Before the mustache can speak, Antwerp blurts out "Hey, man. I know you! I'd recognize that 'stache anywhere!" He turns the camera around to a two-shot of the mustache and Joan holding hands.

The mustache stands craggy and silent, holding back a branch with his free hand, Doctor Livingstone, I presume-ish. He cannot help but stare at the empty wine bottles, the stacked dishes, the fuddled faces. There, but for the intervening decades, goeth he.

"We're making a documentary," says Joan. "Remember?"

"I thought you were getting interviews for the news," the mustache says.

"Oh, that. Yeah, well. We changed our mind," Antwerp says from behind the camera.

"Of course. You're allowed to do that. So who is the documentary about?"

"John K.!" shouts bleary Rupert, waving his green-stained fingers in the air with glee.

"Really," says the mustache. "John K.?"

"Your son. Remember?" says Joan. Her eyes are half-closed.

"I remember. A documentary about John. That's…interesting."

"He's everyman with a microphone and five minutes. The perfect example of what we would all be if we were just given the stage."

"I don't know…" says the mustache, giving his head a little shake. But there's nothing to be gained by thinking too deeply about it. "Would you like to meet him?"

"Boy, would I!" says Joan, as if she hadn't just been introduced to John K. a moment earlier.

It takes a minute or so just to navigate both Antwerp and Joan back to the table where John K. and the others are sitting. Allen and Rupert remain behind to protect the litter of bottles and plates. Joan has two more fingers of greenness in her glass and is sitting again in the mustache's chair. She grips the old microphone in the other, where it sways back and forth like a palm tree in a gale. Antwerp is still rolling, although no one could possibly say what he is recording at this point. Something Warhol might be proud of, perhaps. He sits in the chair the mustache just procured, so the older man finds one more for himself.

"You're him," Joan says, poking John K. with a fingernail leading back to the mic. "He?"

"Him," he corrects, but not actually sure what grammar he is copyediting. The young woman is soggy and drunk and somehow seems to know his father. It is mystery, with a fair amount of screwball, much like a Billy Wilder movie.

"We talked about you."

"We, who?"

"Whom," Joan says breathily, and John K. nods. *Touché!*

"You're the prodigal son of a bitch," she says, and he blinks. "Your dad with a mustache says he's here to watch your bit, your gig, whatever it's called. That's nice, isn't it?"

"Yes," says John K., recognizing that the evening has certain dreamlike qualities to it, with disconnects and coincidences abounding.

"But you don't want him here."

"Hang on. Who said that?" John K. asks, one eyebrow up.

Joan ponders his question a moment.

"No one," she admits, sheepishly.

"Ahh."

"Do you want him here?" she asks, imagining it to be a deft recovery.

"No. Not really."

"And why not?" John K. has a handsome face, not perfect, not young and clear-eyed, but still handsome. The mustache would probably be handsome, too, if she could find out his name. Something in the universe wants him to remain semi-anonymous. Or semi-autonomous. One of those.

He gives her a look, deep and thoughtful, and she bathes in it.

81

"I don't want anyone here," John K. offers. "It's not...funny. Or it's funny, but not amusing."

"Wait a minute," Joan interrupts. "That's the same thing."

"Is it?"

"Isn't it?"

"Let's put a stake in the ground," John K. says. "Like... say, when you're in the shower and you drop something and you bend over to pick it up and your bare butt hits the cold tile of the shower wall. You flinch away and your head hits the door of the shower and it pops open and now you're splashing water all over the bathroom floor so you yank the door shut with soap in your eyes and slam it on your own fingers."

"Yikes," Joan says, but she's smiling. A little bit cross-eyed from the green stuff. Absent. She wants to tell him she doesn't have a shower door.

"Your damn right, yikes. Funny but not amusing. We live in the age of insult. Everything assaults everyone, constantly. It's not a good thing to do. We've become...desensitized to what we say to one another. How is that entertaining? Why don't I get up there and just hit...what's his name with the flat of a shovel? How would that be any different than all the things that everyone is up there saying?"

His voice is quiet, but insistent. In her muddled, beyond-tipsy head, Joan feels like the words are a wave washing over her, bumping her around on the sandy beach, simultaneously pleasing and uncomfortable. She bites back the urge to explain how it's different. Maybe we say stuff so that we won't do stuff. We must experience the worst of the funny because it's necessary.

She thinks about a time when she was driving up from Atlantic City – lousy weather like they only have in New Jersey, cold, rain, dark, and all odors gone-over to rot. The road was slick and there was traffic. There's always traffic. In the tangle of on and off ramps at the Raritan River Bridge, she slowed to take the correct exit, come around and head west when she saw the flashing lights, red and blue, that foretold an accident ahead. Rubberneckers getting their fill before accelerating away. And, of course, she looked, too. You can't not look. We must be hard-wired for it or something.

Police cars. Fire trucks. Klieg lamps illuminating the scene. Men in uniforms, moving urgently. An Econoliner van with its roof sheared off, crumpled back when it had t-boned a jack-knifed tractor-trailer. Passengers in the van – front, second row, third row. A van with a church name painted proudly on the side in a fine cursive hand. Maybe a choir. Maybe the youth group. Each person in the van still wearing their seatbelt, their heads all uniformly snapped backwards as if asleep, the evening rain falling on their faces, pooling in their eyes or dripping into their open, surprised mouths. Hiya, God, old buddy old pal. Got a question for you. What's the point with wearing our fucking seatbelts? Do we get our offering back this week? This is heav-en, huh? So, must we eat with the Presbyterians?

Sometimes we say horrible stuff so we won't do horrible stuff. So we won't go screaming into the night, or climb a bell tower in Austin. We survive the funny as much as anything.

The memory of the broken-necked bodies is so strong that Joan holds out the microphone for John K. to take and stands up. Looking left and right. If she asks where is the restroom? she'll wretch. She presses her palm to her mouth.

Mustache stands and takes her free hand.

"This way." He pulls her gently towards the Blue Room.

Antwerp moves to follow them, but John K. puts a hand on

his shoulder, shakes his head.

"Is she OK," asks Nicole, an unlit cigarette between her lips.

"Sure, sure," says the Old Man. "She'll be right as rain, tomorrow."

"I don't blame Carroll for inventing Archie Bunker, because he didn't. He's far too erudite to have come up with something so banal, so malodorous as the suburban bigot who hates everyone, including himself. I blame him for insisting on doing a good job. He is the one who turned Archie into a loveable grumpy blue-collar type, with no filter between his thoughts and his fat mouth. Really, why couldn't he just put in a half-assed day like everyone else in America. Show up late, take the grief from the director, do a couple of lines of white-powder, blow his lines, and go home to sleep it off. No, he had to be fucking brilliant, believable, real. So that every cracker south of the Battery looked over at their own grandpa and started calling him the Greatest Generation, forgetting that he wasn't the mostly good-natured and sweet-loudmouth Ralph Kramden, but that prick of a bus driver who told Jackie Robinson to move to the back and Rosa Parks to get the hell out of her seat or he'd throw her off himself. Archie is everyone's old man who was a conductor on the Erie-Lackawanna who bitched about his flat feet each evening until his wife finally downed a handful of Miltowns and washed out her brain."

Joan shivers and spits what she hopes is the last bit of mess coming out of her mouth. Nothing says you've gone too far more than a whole lot of green-colored spew pouring out of you into a toilet bowl.

"I want to go home," she mutters to herself.

"Me, too," rumbles a voice behind her, which at first she

attributes to god, but then realizes she's heard the voice before. She still dares not turn around. But if it's the supreme being, creator of the universe, it would be rude not to.

The mustache. Sitting on a footstool. Oh. Well.

"Should you be in the ladies' room?"

"There's no ladies' room. You're in the men's room. It's OK. I'll chase anyone out who tries to interrupt you." His voice is still gravelly, still humorless, but it is finally…friendly? On her side, so to speak. Best she could hope for.

Joan closes her eyes. Her head spins just the least bit, but then it stops. Odd how throwing up fixes so many things. On the other hand, what is she kneeling in on the linoleum in a men's bathroom. She pushes that consideration away.

"Holy shit," she mutters.

"Perfect slapstick. Timing couldn't be better."

"I made a fool out of myself, didn't I?"

"Of course. So what? Who hasn't tonight?" He speaks slowly and quietly. "Welcome to the Club."

It is a cold comfort. But the dizziness is gone and she reaches up to pull some toilet paper to wipe her mouth. Stops, her hand just short of the roll, then shakes her head and yanks it hard so only one tiny sheet snaps off. Fuck. It would be so much better if he weren't here, so she could decide how to clean herself off without an audience. Maybe completely flush her head down the bowl and be done with it. More carefully, she grabs a wad and wipes. Turns and sits on the floor, dignity be damned.

"We are strange creatures," the mustache says into the vomit stink. "We protect and sacrifice with equal abandon. There isn't someone at that table who wouldn't have leapt up to help you. I just got there first. Maybe it's some archaic chivalry bullshit, good teamwork, or just force of habit. And still we will all make fun of you when you return, as soon as we know you're all right. That's the way it is. You know that already, don't you?"

"Where is John K.'s mother?" She blurts it out, because she's been curious about this for a while. As curious as she is about his name.

The mustache doesn't respond immediately.

"You would think that she left us a long time ago, and we're two grown men trying to be adults in the same world, despite our differing views. Or that she passed away when he was a kid, and I wasn't good at raising him. Or maybe you're not thinking anything like that at all." The mustache chews on his words. "Nothing like that. No drama. She's home, doesn't like coming into the city."

"Are you proud of him?"

"That's one of those yes or no questions again. Remember, I said to avoid them, because I can just grunt any old answer and you're stuck with lousy footage."

Joan looks around, holds up her hands in a shrug.

"No camera here, my friend. Just answer."

"Yes. I'm proud of him. But mostly for still being here."

Joan wants to know more but doesn't ask. That'll have to do.

She carefully clambers to her feet and pads to the sink, rinsing out her mouth, splashing her face and looks at herself in the little mirror. Hair is a train-wreck, but happily unfouled by frog colored vomit. Good enough. The mustache stands and pulls an ironically green packet of Doublemint from his trousers pocket, holds it out to her.

"Thank you. Do we have to go back out there?" Joan asks. She pushes her wet hands through her hair. How she must look…

"Baby sister, this is comedy," the mustache says. "You take the good with the bad."

◆◆◆

# 9

Allen and Rupert have emerged from behind the potted plant and joined them, sharing a chair, a complete flat of breakfast crumb-cake, unsliced, and an open magnum of medium-quality champagne and some red-solo cups they've pilfered. They've been busy little drunk beavers.

The Dean of Friars arrives at the table, arms akimbo, his face an angry red. He is beside himself. Everyone is drinking out of plastic cups. They are all eating…what the hell is that? Breakfast?

"Why didn't you tell me that you needed a bigger table?" he snipes at The Old Man, who doesn't bother to answer that question.

"My friend, are you going to join us or be pissed that we're having a better time than you?"

"I'm busy," the Dean says, petulantly.

"Last chance," says the Old Man. "I won't ask you again. And you haven't even met Nicole here, and she doesn't know any of your stories. It's the shank of the evening. You choose to be cranky and leave, you'll regret it…"

The Dean of Friars sees the world crystal-clearly for that absolutely perfect moment, feels the singularity, and snatches a chair for himself, sitting between the Old Man and the very pretty young woman. The table is now a complete madhouse. Allen pours some champagne in a solo cup for the Dean, who takes it, gives him a look, and mouths a silent thank-you. Without saying a word, they know they need to talk to each other tomorrow, but about what neither has quite decided, yet.

The current roaster calls loudly for John K. to come up to the podium. At the mic'd sound of his name, everyone at the table turns and looks at him, frozen in anticipation. He stands and the chair nearly tips over. A low chuckle waves around the room for the near-pratfall.

"Holy shit," John K. says from the podium, bending over a little to get the right audio response from the microphone. The electronics sing a feedback tune and then silence.

He can tell that this is suddenly a hostile crowd, tired of the night, tired of trying to laugh at everything whether it deserves their laughter or not, and way past time to wrap it all up. He should have left, earlier. No, no. Gotta do it. Gotta persevere. Apache is right. Sometimes you walk right into the lion's mouth.

"Fuck, 'em," says the mustache, his growl loud enough to be heard. "Fuck 'em if they can't take a joke." Another chuckle wavelet.

"I've no interest at all in talking about Carroll O'Connor," John K. says, his words soft despite being amplified through the speakers. "Is that going to be a problem? I know you paid… absolutely nothing to be here, so I really didn't plan to give a shit about your opinion at all, but you should be aware that I was asked to be more polite than I have been before. And for those of you who know me, that's a pretty large leap of faith."

He takes a deep breath and exhales a sigh into the mic.

"My name is John K. and I'm an addict."

Some folks in the audience shout *Hi, John K.!* because they know from their own experience that you should, even if just from muscle-memory. This is it. Antwerp points the camera, adjusts his headphones and Joan holds out the mic for him. He can hear it picking up John K.'s voice just fine and nods, giving her a thumbs up.

"I know that's why we're here, why you're here, but I'm sorry, but I really don't feel like insulting our roastee tonight. Or, I'm not sorry. I can tell you're all tired of it, and like I said, I'm just not in the mood. But I have the podium and five or so minutes to burn, so I'm going to stay up here. What to talk about, though?

"You know, a smart guy once wrote that by now we were supposed to already have a colony orbiting in space. In case you haven't noticed, we don't. And I've been thinking lately about how things start. How habits, our traditions, begin. What are the backstories? The origins. What are our mythologies? Take comedy, for instance. How did comedy first happen? Can it be so simple as some poor slob falling down a hill above a frozen lake during the ice age and spinning and sliding in a panic until he ended up coming to a stop in front of a dire wolf? Slapstick? Or was he flopping around on the ice and one wolf batted at him when he came close and sent him ricocheting around on the ice to another wolf, who swatted him with a paw, sending him back to the first wolf, who batted him around again. Like they invented hockey. Slapstick slapshot. Oh, and when they finally got bored, the wolves fucking ate him.

"Doesn't that seem plausible? Think about your own dog and your nice living room sofa. Now leave your dog inside and go to work, or even just outside to mow the lawn. Your dog gets bored. You finally come home. So, how's that couch doing now?

"But you're right, you're right. I don't think comedy began like that, either. Actually, I imagine it being when one of the first people – proto-men, if you will – tried to get everyone's attention about something. This one fellow, let's call him Oog – well, nobody ever listens to him. You know what I mean - he's not the biggest or strongest in his clan, didn't discover how to defend a water hole, and they're all sitting around the fire, chewing on something they hunter-gathered – and Oog's trying to talk during this family dinner about how he'd seen something he found noteworthy earlier in the day. A great lake of melted ice, above their camp. But the tribe, they're all who cares? There are giant crocodiles and mastodons all over the damned place. It's prehistoric times, for crap's sake. Oog, you talk too fucking much. And they ignore him and yell for someone to pass the hunk of salt.

"But our guy Oog is genuinely concerned about what he'd seen. So he stands up on a rock and starts shouting his news, over the chatter and grunting and chewing. And now he has their attention. What the fuck? they mutter to each other. They listen for a moment, because he's shouting about – the ice melting or some other nonsense – but he's spoiling the overall dinner vibe. One of his cohorts, he's heard this before, because Oog always has a conspiracy about the ice melting or evolution or something, finds a pile of somewhat fresh Woolly Mammoth crap outside the cave opening near a bush. He's not Oog's brightest contemporary, and mistakes what he's picked up for a rock, which he'd planned to throw at Oog. He snatches up a piece and it crumbles in his hand and so of course he gives it the sniff-test, and yes, indeed, it's not a rock but a massive Mammoth dump. Not what he originally wanted, but it will do. And he flings it at Oog, from the back of the cave room and it sprinkles all over everything,

91

the people, the dinner they're eating and smacks Oog square in the chest.

"Not that they'd even invented the square yet, but you get my point.

"So, now Oog has Mammoth shit all over himself, and a bruised chest, but he's still trying to tell what he's seen, and how they're in grave danger. But everyone in the room is sort of mad at him for standing up, because he's ruining supper, and they're also mad at him because he got shit thrown at him that also got all in the food and their hair and clothes, such as they were, like that was somehow also directly his fault. But they're also laughing, because Oog has Mammoth shit on him and it's funny because it smells really bad now. Bad, even for cavemen. Or maybe they smell Mammoth shit everywhere and see it on him, so it must be him that really, really stinks.

"Don't ask me why that's funny.

"And Oog can't even hear himself over the noise of his family and friends. He stands there, silent and crap-besmeared.

"And, naturally, someone else gets in on the act. One of the younger family members finds the pile of crumbling shit and throws it at Oog. He misses him, and the Mammoth-pie hits someone else in the face. Which is also funny. Classically so. Then that poor slob goes and grabs some crap, of course, and throws it at the younger fellow and soon shit is flying all around the cave. Because it's disgusting, and so it's also funny. Anyone still laughing is fair game for a handful of shit in the face. The shitfaced ones throw Mammoth pie at the ones who aren't yet shitfaced.

"Oog sits down, because there's nothing else left for him to do. He told them the truth. He told them the truth, and they laughed. He slept the fear-of-being-eaten-by-cave-bears sleep of the just. And, of course, in the next day or so the lake of water broke through the dam of ice and came down in a giant torrent and wiped out their camp, killing most of the clan. Oog, who knew this was going to happen, was perched on top of a tall hill and saw it all go down, shaking his head that no one cared that he'd told them the truth. Only that he made them laugh. The moral of the story being that sometimes in comedy your shit stinks and sometimes you kill.

"And sometimes your audience is shitfaced, and, as we all know, you can't do a damned thing about that. And just sometimes, you're king of the hill."

He stands back from the mic to a trickle of laughter and applause. So it goes.

Antwerp clicks off the camera. The battery is dead. There's another battery, but it's in the van. Well, he hopes that he caught it all. The roast is over. He wonders where Carroll O'Connor even is. It might have made sense to have a one shot of him, all wispy-white haired and laughing at the event. Or sleeping. Or angry. Whichever.

The jazz combo squeaks to life again, and John K. returns, sits down at the table. No one says anything for a while. Finally, before the timing is spoiled, the mustache leans over and claps him once on the shoulder. The Dean of Friars nods. The Old Man gives him a wink.

There you are. As with many New York traditions, they fizzle after a big finale. New Year's Eve? You'll still have to catch the subway home. Last year, the Yankees beat the Mets and won the World Series! So what? It's another season and, well, shit...I got nothin'. A roast? After everyone shoots their wad, you still need a quiet corner of someplace to ride out your impending hangover.

"We're going to the Drake."

"The Drake? That dump? Should we get a cab? Wait. You think they have a couple of extra rooms?"

"Probably. It's two blocks up. We can walk there."

"Is it still raining?"

"I don't know. Go outside and look up. They say it's gonna be nice tomorrow."

"Ah, what does the weatherman know?" Everyone snickers.

Joan hands the mic to Antwerp. It's time to leave.

"I'll walk you to the door," says John K.

"Thanks."

The place is quieter, subdued, but it seems like everyone is getting a last drink under their belt. They meander between the tables to the front door. One or two give John K. a smile, a nod.

September is New York's best month. Don't let anyone tell you otherwise. And it's nice out for a Monday night. The tenth. Or is it the eleventh? On this street, at this time of night there are times when you can see a star or two in the sky.

He doesn't want to ask. Asks anyway.

"How do you think I did?"

Joan smiles.

"How do you think you did?"

He finds he doesn't have an answer. In the end, what his father calls the grand scheme of things, he doesn't really care. That has to be good, right?

"You OK to drive?" John K. asks. Joan shrugs.

"I don't know. Antwerp is the driver." The cameraman is at the van, carefully putting everything in cases, and stowing them in their proper spots. "If we have to, we'll just tilt the seats back and catch a few zees, let the pain kick in and then head back to

the office. It's too late to do anything else, and too early to get
fired."

John K. gives her a noncommittal mm-hmm, like he's interviewing her. Turnabout is fair play.

"You could go with my father and the others over to the
Drake."

"You don't think they'd mind?" She likes the mustache.
She likes him more because he's not…dangerous. Everything is
better when people just decide on being friends.

"Nah. Everyone will be camping out, beds and couches.
Pop will find an old movie on TV, even though it's way too late
to stay up. Then they'll break into the mini-fridges, do some real
damage to cheesy crackers and little chocolate donuts. Probably
charge it to the Friars Club."

"Oh, my," Joan says, at a loss. "And what about you?"
She almost makes a face at herself because of how it sounds.

"Me?" He looks around, like he can figure things out by
triangulating where he is in the universe, then make a calculated
decision. "I think I'm heading downtown."

"Can we give you a ride?" she asks, sheepishly.

"One of you two driving? God, no, thank you." John K.
laughs, then laughs harder because it's only the first time he's
laughed today. Or is it finally tomorrow? He doesn't look at his
Faux-lex, because, well, why fucking bother?

He'll stroll over to Broadway and find a cab going downtown. He shakes her hand. Heads west.

95

Garrison Somers is an editor and author
living with his wife in Chapel Hill, NC.

www.ingramcontent.com/pod-product-compliance
Lightning Source LLC
Chambersburg PA
CBHW070347130626
46556CB00007B/3066